# LANCELOT: THE CORNWALL CHAPTERS

## NICHOLAS T. MORROW

This is a work of fiction. The events and characters described herein are imaginary and are not intended to refer to specific places or living persons. The opinions expressed in this manuscript are solely the opinions of the author and do not represent the opinions or thoughts of the publisher. The author has represented and warranted full ownership and/or legal right to publish all the materials in this book.

Lancelot: The Cornwall Chapters
All Rights Reserved.
Copyright © 2013 Nicholas T. Morrow
v3.0

This book may not be reproduced, transmitted, or stored in whole or in part by any means, including graphic, electronic, or mechanical without the express written consent of the publisher except in the case of brief quotations embodied in critical articles and reviews.

Outskirts Press, Inc.
http://www.outskirtspress.com

ISBN: 978-1-4787-0555-0

Outskirts Press and the "OP" logo are trademarks belonging to Outskirts Press, Inc.

PRINTED IN THE UNITED STATES OF AMERICA

# Preface

If by some chance that a soul is reading these last words by me, I must thank the Father, my God, for bestowing me this mercy even past death. I, of all people know how cruel the passage of time can be towards men. Things that once stood erected proudly for display are withered away by the passing sands. Buildings, homes, kingdoms, ideals, promises, and loyalties: none of these can escape from its clutches and history is no exception as well. Even in my old age nearly fifty years after certain events I can see the tales that I once lived myself changing form and context as they leap from person to person. I am known to be the noblest of all knights and the greatest warrior our land has ever known. Such things are nothing but falsehoods that have spun out of control over time. There was indeed once greatness in my life, but I squandered it all away on the trivialities of my flesh. I write down the excerpts of my life so that once history has forgotten the truth of the world. I may serve to remind them of the follies of men and how the selfish desires of the heart can destroy even the greatest kingdoms. But all things have a starting point…

*These are the words of Lancelot De Luc, the destroyer of Camelot.*

## Chapter One
# The Lady of the Lake

**THE KEY WAS** balance. With each step I took, I had to ensure that my fingers always maintained their position under the center of the tray. When I had first began serving the vagabonds that visited the brothel, the tray would easily slide across the smooth layers that were once the tips of my fingers. But what had once been skin liken to that of a newborn babe was replaced with blistered fingertips that were able to perfectly control the tray on most occasions. With that said, I still found it to be paramount that I maintained that perfect balance. If they ventured too far to the left of the tray, or if they scurried too much to the right, then all chaos would break out. The heat from the stew was making its way to the tips of my fingers which made me hurry my pace across the floor, but not too much because the last time I rushed myself one of our patrons ended up living true to his nickname of *Red Leg* Drake. The burns weren't half as bad as they seemed at first glance, but he insisted that I pay with my life. It only took a few moments after I drew my sword for him to reconsider how rude he had been. That's how it was with most of these sad excuses for fighters and warriors. If you believed half of the nonsense sprouting from their mouths, you'd think them able to go toe to toe with King Uther, but when it actually came time to prove their worth they always find a way to make a fool of themselves.

I placed their food right between the cluttered pile of empty mugs and cards and to their great dismay tore down their stockade of mugs that Stenos had been assembling for the last hour. I had to hold my breath the entire time as the rank smell of liquor tried its hardest to kill me, but thank God I had become quite proficient at this or else Mother would be without her precious, darling Lancelot. Once I had collected what I needed, I took my leave without delay and then suddenly received a hard slap across my buttocks. I held back my initial desire to draw my dagger and just walked away. Either those men were so far gone that they mistook me for one of the serving wenches or they have some weird tastes.

I looked over at Roland who was serving across the room. Our eyes met and I signaled him that I had now delivered twenty-one meals without a single spill: a new record for the brothel. He dismissed my gesture and returned back to work. I swear he could be such a stiff sometimes it was suffocating.

A loud crash could be heard back towards the kitchen and I rushed in that direction. Just as I had expected was Luciana was on the floor covered with shattered dishes, stew, and mead all over her. It was a fine look for her in my opinion considering how well the cranberry sauce brought out the color in her eyes. I took out my hand towel and dowsed it in some dishwater as I began to clean her face. She had that pathetic look on her face as tears were slowly accumulating in her eyes. I tried to wipe her tears but only found myself getting my own hands sticky from whatever else she had managed to spill on herself. After taking another look at her, I figured it would just be best for her to wash in the lake. I took her hand and we left out of the back door while everyone else was busy attending to the various foods we cooked such as roasts, rice, stew, and whatever else Lord Julian wanted us to make.

The night was young as we exited the building into the grassy meadows that stretched onward until it reached the shore of the island. The blades of grass tickled my legs as the wind slightly pushed them along the rolling green meadow. Luciana took a firm grip of my hand as she led me to the shoreline of the island. The water from the lake skirted across the shore as it crept slowly towards our sandy feet before it quickly retreated back to the bulk of the sea. I felt Luciana's hand slip through mine as she pranced into the water without a care in the world. It always amazed me that she was considered to be three years older than me when in truth she often acted like a child. As she proceeded deeper into the waters, I took a seat a safe distance away from the rolling waves and took a glance back at the shining lights from the brothel. The island was a small one that left little room for anything else aside from the brothel, so even from the shore of the island I could see that rocking wooden sign of *The Lady of Lake* swaying in the wind.

My observation was interrupted when that foolish girl decided to attack me with a continuous barrage of water she kept splashing on me. If she thought I would allow her to get away with such a dishonorable attack, she had another thing coming. With one powerful sweep of my hand through the water, I threw a wave of cold water upon her and the two of us engaged in a frivolous game that we had played with one another since we were children. When she finally stopped, I hardly had any time to react to her pouncing on me like some sort of animal. The water from our game had well seeped into her clothing and dripped down onto me as her body was pressed against mine in the sand. Her soft lips found soon their way to mine as she pinned me down. My eyes closed by instinct and I found myself kissing her back.

Luciana Aubrey, she was the first of many for me: my first friend, my first kiss, and the first and only person I could actually trust at that time. We had known each other for as long as I could remember since we had both been subjected to the life of living in this brothel since we were able to walk. Only she knew the hardships and the shame that was instilled into my heart, and she was the only soul that could help alleviate my sorrows. Her lips departed from mine as she rested her head on my chest. I twirled her silky black hair around my finger as the waves tickled our feet. The sweet smell of the lake mixed in with her natural aroma put a smile on my face that was long overdue those days. My smile faded as she left me and stared out at our watery bedside. She had done that a lot lately: every now and then the outside world around her would disappear and she would gaze off as she sank into her own world full of worries.

It was hard to blame her though, she had just recently turned sixteen and she would now be considered a woman.

Well if truth be told she had already been considered a woman because of how mature her body had developed that last year. No longer was she the flat tomboy that used to swim with me off of the shore. She had now become the desire of every scoundrel and man that came to the brothel and within just a couple of days she would be available for purchase. The idea of some fat, old drunkard laying his filthy hands all over her body was enough to send me into a rage, but I could do nothing but watch and one day collect the coins spent on her.

*The world is a dark place and the only light in it is the shine of a gold coin.*

Those were the words my mother told me when I first learned of her life as nothing but a common whore and how I was just the son of a whore. She told me that if I hated her life so badly then I should leave because she was doing this in order to keep me alive. Unfortunately, Luciana would have to accept the same fate for herself. A cool wind blew my hair across my eyes. I parted the wet jet-black strands out of the way as I got up and reached for Luciana. Her hand slipped into mine once more as she followed me back to the brothel. She stopped once we reached the back door and her grip around my hand tightened. She looked me in the eye with those piercing eyes of hers. Her cheeks began to redden as she awkwardly asked me, "Lancelot…I…I want you to be my first."

I wish that I had been born with the naiveté that most boys my age had because then I would have no idea what she meant. I felt my own face began to redden as I thought of the possibility of us together. It was not as if Luciana and I had never been somewhat intimate together, but even on occasions like what had just happened on the shore were all looked at as us just messing around. We had always been like that with one another for as long as I could remember. Luciana had an inherent curious nature when it came to things, and her own body was no such exception. I suppose growing up in a brothel produced either one of two results: either one would hate the life that surrounds him or he would just succumb to it and begin to revel in the exotic pleasantries that life brings with it. In her case it was definitely the latter. She never looked at the women in the brothels as low class whores without an ounce of dignity. If anything, she respected them for living such a life while maintaining a smile on their faces. She always knew that one day she would have to wear that same smile on her face, so she figured that she might as well get as much practice as possible, but I had never imagined she would want to go this far.

I replied. "Luciana what are you talking about?"

She let go of my hand and backed away while making that pouting face she had become a master at since she was five.

"Don't feign ignorance and innocence with me Lancelot! You know what I mean. Soon…very soon I will become just another tool for Lord Julian to profit off of. I have made my peace with that long ago, but I don't want my maidenhood ripped away by some sleazy vagabond for a few copper pieces!" She walked closer to me and began to blush once more as she took my hands within hers. "I've known you all of my life, and thus I know that your eyes have finally matured and that they have a taste for me. Even when you make your jests towards me I can see that in your heart you have other intentions. And you've developed into a fine young man yourself. Even among the older women, talk of your comeliness is spreading. Years from now I want to be able to look back and at least say I gave myself to someone worth respect."

I looked at her whole body and realized it would be a lie if I denied my desire for her. Even as we merely played around time and time again with our kisses and laying together, I always knew that a part of me wanted her. Those feelings became apparent not long ago as I saw her bathe in the lake. I pulled away from her as my eyes shifted towards the ground.

Without looking her in the eye still, I found myself replying with a strong tone, "Lucy, I have no intention on becoming nothing more than a saddle to ease your ride into your new life."

I turned away to the sound of her sobs as I walked back into the brothel to finish the night's work.

The rest of the night went without any further incidents, so I was able to leave the rest of my duties to Roland as I went downstairs to the *Siren's Nest* to say goodnight to my mother. The *Siren's Nest* was the heart of the *Lady of the Lake*. The whole floor was draped with silk curtains and exotic rugs bought from Persian merchants. A sweet fragrance lingered down the hall that enticed any man to pursue his deepest desires. I hated having to venture down this way because even though I couldn't see it I knew of the immoral actions taking place behind these doors. Even behind closed doors I could hear the moans of many of the women who had helped raise me as they sold their dignity off for a few pieces of so called "light". The sounds only made me wish to leave this place as soon as possible but I found myself pausing as I looked at the newly decorated door with Luciana's name upon the door. The door had been draped with freshly cut flowers from the meadows outside to indicate she was fresh meat for anyone interested. I pushed the door open and saw the room where my best friend would be treated as a tool for the ruffians that strolled through there like they owned the place.

How could such a beautiful room signify such a disgusting fate that awaited her? I wished to see no more of that room and I continued my trip to Mother's room.

As usual, I had impeccable timing as a half naked man came out of her room with a disgusting grin on his face. He looked down at me and rubbed my head. His hands were sweaty and reeked of fish and waste. A common pirate no doubt. As he buckled his trousers, he laughed at me.

"Well kid, I'd say you were a bit too young for her but what the hell. You're never too young for the treasures a whore has stashed away."

I didn't say a word to the likes of him as I walked into Mother's room and slammed the door shut behind me. It must have not been too long since she was done entertaining her client because she was still in full uniform as she lay on her bed. The candlelight made her sandy Persian skin glow like a flawless gem. It was common knowledge in the brothel that Mother was the most beautiful of all the women there. With her glowing skin, doe like eyes, and exotic wild black hair, she was able to easily claim that title since she was a young girl of eighteen.

When her eyes met mine, they had no shame in them. She had long ago succumbed to the nature of the life she was a prisoner of. She slowly got up and wrapped a robe around herself as she opened up her arms waiting for her darling Lancelot to fall into them as I had once eagerly done as a boy. In order to make her happy, I complied with her request and embraced her. She smelt of rotten fish and liquor. I nearly pushed her away but I calmed myself. I could still remember her face the last time I had done such a thing. She let me go as she went to brush her hair in the mirror. I came behind her and took the brush away from her hand and proceeded to do it for her. I used to always love brushing Mother's hair to make her as beautiful as possible.

She placed her hand on mine and turned around to look me eye to eye. She rested her hand on my cheek as she said, "Lancelot, don't you think it would be better for you to be brushing Lucy's hair instead. This will be her last night she has a bed to herself."

Her words were cold but they were the hard truth. Once I had saw the new door moments ago, my heart dropped as I thought of what she would have to endure tomorrow. I thought back to how insensitive my words had been to her when in all truth I did not mean what I had said.

Right when I was about to say something, a knock was heard at her door. The thump occurred three times. One knock meant food; two knocks meant friend; and three knocks only meant client. I took my leave as Mother put back on her uniform. I looked back at her as the warm doe like eyes I had seen a moment ago faded to cold ones devoid of emotion. On the floor where the tavern resided, all was quiet as the only customers left were passed out either in their own vomit or in a corner somewhere. Roland was busy sweeping and I passed by and just gave a courteous smile. I tried my best to proceed up the stairs to the third floor quietly but with each step I took, the stairs under me creaked. Despite the amount of money we brought in, the only nice part of *The Lady of the Lake* was *The Siren's Nest*. The rest of the brothel was just a shabby piece of construction thrown together.

On the top floor, there were only three rooms. One was Lord Julian's office for whenever he stopped by. I had only been in there once and I still remember how brightly the room shined with all of the coins he had littered all over the place. The other room while not nearly as decorated was my own. It was a quaint abode with nothing to decorate the small space but a mat on the floor and my collection of swords and daggers that our patrons often left behind by mistake. The other room was Luciana's but that one would soon be used for gambling den as Lord Julian had planned. Her room was far bigger than mine and it even had an armoire to boot. It was said that this room and all of the lush décor associated with it was a gift from Luciana's late parents. I knew nothing of her parents save the fact that they abandoned her at the doorstep of the brothel fifteen years ago.

Her door was closed as I approached it. Normally I would have just barged in without a care, but this time I knocked three times.

## Chapter Two
# Lancelot De Luc

**THERE ARE SOME** things in life that can change a man for the best or for the worst. I can say that without a doubt that my choice to share that night with Luciana was one of those fateful decisions. To this day I wish that I had been able to just sever my attachment to her and continue on with my life, but such willpower has never been a strong suit of mine in the first place. As I look back on that night, I have yet to discover what was it that made me become so attached to her to such a degree. The one thing that I did discover that night is that I finally understood why brothels were such a coveted place to go.

The following morning I awoke to nothing but a sea of long raven hair in my face. As I moved it out of the way, I was greeted by perhaps the most angelic face I have witnessed in my lifetime. Her mouth was slightly parted as I traced my finger around it and placed a kiss on her forehead. A sweet smile crept on her face as she slowly opened her eyes. I ran my hand along the side of her body as I kissed her good morning. Her arms wrapped around my body as I pulled her closer to me. I found myself gripping onto her tighter and tighter as I thought back to how beautiful our night was together. In a fit of unprecedented rage, I threw her off of me and got up from the bed right as the tears came streaming down my face.

I couldn't control it. Anger and the sadness came and wrapped thier cold fingers around my heart and their grip wouldn't ease up. I looked back at Luciana and marveled at how beautiful she looked as the rays of the sun made her skin glisten. She came and wrapped her arms around me as I stared out at the lake. The water was as still as my heart at that moment as I clutched tightly onto the window and continued to cry. I found my sorrow broken when I heard Luciana say, "I'm sorry that I asked you to do that Lancelot. It was a selfish request and for that…"

The ludicrous idea of me being sorrowful because of that night made me kiss her to shut her up. When our lips said their final goodbyes, I laughed as I told her, "What happened last night was the greatest thing in my life Lucy."

I wrapped my arms around her waist and kissed her forehead once more. I wiped away my tears as I continued to ease her worries, "These tears were shed because…because I don't understand why my father could share a moment like the one we had with my mother and then leave. I don't know how any man can prance in here pay for such a beautiful thing and then cast the memory away as if it were nothing but an exquisite meal."

She pressed her head against my chest and tightened her own grip around me.

"Your father was a soldier Lancelot, and a foreign soldier at that."

"I know that. I have heard the tale too often of how a comely Roman Centurion came in here wounded and on the verge of death and how a simple serving girl that had no intention to becoming a whore tended to his wounds and took him into her parent's house, a Persian camp where they restored him to health. The great Centurion repaid that woman by giving her a child and leaving her in the den of night because Romans viewed Persians as a worthless people that deserved nothing but death or servitude, and the thought of being the father of one shamed him too much. From that day my mother was forced to work in this filthy place because her parents refused to help her now that she carried a half-breed in her." I looked into her eyes and stroked her hair. "I will never leave you like he did. I'll stand by you and…"

She pulled away from me as those words were uttered out of my mouth. As I took a step closer to her, she slapped me with the full force of her hand.

"How dare you say such a thing to me today of all days! How dare you of all people try to break the resolve that I have to do this! Last night wasn't an act of love, but rather an act of pride to myself. I thought that you of all people would understand that and not fill your head with fanciful illusions of us being together. This is the world we live in Lancelot! Have you learned nothing from the sacrifice Vivian, your mother has made for you?"

"I have learned from her, and because of her sacrifice I now know that I don't ever want to be like her and I don't want you to be like her!"

"Well when you create a perfect world where the poor

and destitute don't have to sell themselves to live then I won't be like her."

Tears were now running down her face as it turned to a harsh red pigment that matched the harshness of her words.

> *The world is full of darkness and the only light*
> *in the world is the shine of a coin.*

Before she became even more infuriated with me, I took my leave and returned to my own room. Her words stayed with me though as I looked upon my fine collection of blades that hung on my wall. The Sun had already reached a point where the room was filled with its light, so the dull steel glowed radiantly in the sunlight. I took a hold of my first blade that I had found on the body of a mercenary that lost a dual. As I took the blade into my hand, my nerves were eased just as they always were. The handle had a warm touch to it as if Mother herself had taken a hold of my hand. It was a Gladius, a type of short sword, that most likely belonged to a slain Roman. The steel had a good balance to it that made it easy even for someone my size and age to handle with some skill. I thought of the pure irony that perhaps this blade belonged to my father due to its Roman background. My mother's warm embrace and my father's heritage: it was because of these two things, which made this blade my favorite. I twirled the blade around a couple of times and stabbed at the air as if Lord Julian was there himself. I had often thought of simply killing him with one of these blades to earn the freedom Mother and I so richly deserved, but the idea had never taken root until now. With Luciana so intent that this way of life was the only one viable, then perhaps I had no choice. Lord Julian was just a low class Roman politician that decided to stay after his people pulled out in hopes of maintaining a profit. No one would miss him if he suddenly were to just vanish.

Throughout history, blades had always been a symbol of freedom for a man as he fought for whatever he believed in. Perhaps that's why I had become so enamored by them at a young age. I have desired nothing but my freedom from this life, and I always believed that to get it I would have to fight for it. I ran my fingers over the steel of the blade and pricked my finger when I touched the point of it. It was the only blade of my collection that was in excellent shape. As I continued to marvel at it, I heard Mother call my name and I quickly realized that I had to be at work soon.

I figured that I was already late and just threw on my clothes from the previous day as I ran downstairs to serve our *esteemed* guests. The moment I hit the floor of the tavern I knew that something was off. The usual songs of plunder and pillaging sung by the worthless scum that came there had been replaced with ballads of men in pristine armor toasting glasses of ale to one another. With armor that had barely had a scratch and blades forged with the finest steel, these men gathered around one another and shared warm smiles as they went on about their exploits. Those men were no doubt the prestigious Britannia Legionnaires under the rule of King Uther. They were said to be the best warriors in all of the newly united lands of Albion and that they had no equal when it came to dancing with their blades.

The moment that I laid my eyes upon the Pendragon

Dragon insignia that was laminated on their armor I knew that I had to be the one to serve them. For years since their formation, I had heard stories of their greatness and now they ate and drank not too far from where I stood. It was difficult to hide my excitement as I went straight to the kitchen to discover who among all of the servers was responsible for taking care of those men and Roland seemed to be the one doing it. Roland was nothing more than a son of a baker from the bandit controlled western land of Cambria looking for any kind of work he was able to find, and that search landed him here in Southern Albion at *The Lady of the Lake*. There was no way he would be able to grasp the magnitude of who he was serving. Such an honor was squandered upon him.

He was a vestige a perfect commoner: he had no real aspirations to guide his life; he cared little for the world around him, and he simply was driven by the need to fill his stomach. I pitied such an existence, but that day I knew I would love him for it. From just a couple of glances from when I first saw the knights, I counted perhaps ten had taken a seat.

On a normal day, the most asked of any server would just be a few men, but ten warriors who would no doubt have a serious appetite because of whatever journey they had just finished would be too much for Roland and he and I both knew that.

When I approached him, he was struggling to stack multiple trays of freshly prepared roast on his arms. Whether it was the steam of the newly made meat that made his brow start to sweat or that he was already that stressed, I could see that he needed my help. The frustration in his face was mounting as he realized that he didn't possess the skill to carry all of the food. It was during this peak moment of doubt that I slipped in and offered him a hand. On any normal day, he would have told me to mind my own business for if there was one thing that Roland did have it was his pride. He always hated the fact that I was better than him at our job, looks, fighting, and that I had captured Luciana's eye in his opinion. I imagined the look on his face once he found out that I had spent the night with her. The thought was almost enough to make me drop one of the plates.

This time we both held our tongues as he tried his best to shackle his pride, and I kept my dirty little secret to myself. There was no urgent need to go and ruin such an amicable relationship between the two of us…yet.

By the time we left the kitchen, the bar was now full of our more common patrons that frequented quite often. It was a peculiar sight to see warriors of such noble prestige forced to eat so closely with the very class of men that they had to fight on a daily basis. Despite the lucrative profits we brought in for Lord Julian, we were still a lowly brothel that only likes of pirates, bandits, and other criminals came to. Due to our more isolated location, it was a rarity to serve anyone of any real prominence, but that day was an exception.

As they drank and danced to their own merriment, I maneuvered my way around them and I continued to press onward to the table holding the Legionnaires. Unfortunately, I failed to take my own advice and was soon hurrying towards the table too fast.

It all happened in an instant. Somehow I lost my balance

and just as I predicted the result was pure chaos. The trays all managed to slip out at the same time and the contents splattered all over one of our better known customers: Isaac, the bull. I quickly remembered that we called him the bull for two reasons. The first one obviously being due to his size, but the second one eluded me until I saw the intensity that had taken over his face. He suddenly swung at me, but I had always been gifted with great reaction time so I was able to avoid the attack. He drew a blade from his side and I drew my dagger.

I took a good look at Isaac and knew within the first few seconds that I could take him with relative ease. Judging from how he swung his arm at me earlier, I could tell that he fought with nothing but power as relative to his namesake. I had already proven that I could dodge him once, so all I needed was one well-placed strike.

That was not the first time that I had managed to get myself into an altercation with one of our patrons. In fact that kind of thing had become somewhat of an expectation around the brothel lately. The regulars around this time in the day had gathered around Isaac and me and soon a ring of death had been formed for the two of us to dance in. Isaac tore off his shirt and threw it to the crowd as he let off an odd roar that I suppose was to either intimidate me or imitate a dying bear.

These kinds of men were always looking for a reason to get into a fight and I was more than happy to give them a reason to leave the brothel. While most boys my age would have been frightened by this sort of predicament, I found myself reveling in the opportunity to once again prove my worth. All of my life I had been brought up in this brothel and taught nothing but how to serve the patrons that frequented here. Because of that, I could easily say that I had no other skills to speak of aside from one: my skill to fight… and to win.

Right before we began, Mother came from downstairs and in no time at all pushed her way through the crowd to get over to me. While I tried my best to avoid having any eye contact with her, my fears came to fruition and our eyes met once more. Her eyes exuded a powerful mixture of sorrow, anger, and sternness all blended into something I could not name. I already knew what she was pleading me to do with all of her heart as she stood there frozen in fear of what I may do. In all of the fights I had gotten into thus far with customers, I had yet to lose one. In most cases though, that meant that we would lose several regulars and the one thing Lord Julian hated was losing money. And if Lord Julian lost any more money because of my fights, then he promised that would be the end of the line for my mother and me here.

Was that such a bad thing though? I hated my life here and if we got thrown out then nothing could hold us back, but Mother was like me and raised in this place so her skills were limited as well. The only job she would be able to find that would keep us alive and well would be that of a whore once more at another brothel, but if we would be tied down to this life no matter what decision I made then why not just choose the one in which we would be free to live how we wanted for a little while.

All I had to do to escape this hell temporarily was to attack, but Mother had it so good here that I truly didn't have it in me to rip her life away from her. I lowered my dagger and griped the handle as hard as I could to get ready for the thrashing I would soon receive. I put my head down as the bull charged me and I waited and waited and waited...I looked up after a second to see that Luciana had gotten between the two of us. It was an odd sight to see such a fragile girl standing as my last line of defense, but there she was with her arms outstretched as if she was ready to take on the world.

Her eyes had a nasty glare in them that actually made Isaac back off to my surprise for a moment. But if she thought that a man of Isaac's reputation would be stopped by a mere girl, then she was just as foolish as always. In an unexpected sudden burst she proclaimed to Isaac, "Don't you dare harm a hair on his head! In exchange...I'll give you me free of charge."

She had said it with such conviction that Isaac actually lowered his blade in submission to her request. Despite how strongly she said it, I could still see past her bravado. Her legs were trembling the entire time as she spoke and I'm sure she had to do her best to hold back her tears. Was this how it was supposed to be? I had done my best to protect Luciana our whole lives and make sure she was happy as her best friend, but now here she was protecting me at the cost of her own body. She knew that if I fought him, then that would be the end of the line for my mother and me. Was she that committed to her new life already that she could barter herself off as a common piece of meat?

Isaac took a good look at her and then cracked back his arm and backhanded her in the face. She dropped to the floor in an instant. It was said that the bull always had a disgusting habit of beating his women first and then taking them.

No second thoughts; no hesitation; no changes. Before he had a chance to ever lay his filthy hand on Luciana or any other woman ever again, I removed it from his possession in one clean-cut from my dagger. Hearing the bull scream like a little girl who had just received a spanking was perhaps one of the most humorous things I have ever heard. He screamed for his friends to come take my head as I stepped in front of Luciana. I knew that Mother and I would be punished for my actions, but for the first time in my life, I felt as if I was doing what I was born to do. I had no hate for Isaac, felt no pity, and harbored no thoughts of my superiority. It was simple: he hurt Luciana and I would not allow him to ever do that again.

Five more men came forward armed with swords that had a look of blood lust in their eyes. I knew that I was a good fighter compared to those guys, but five on one…even I knew that I would not walk away from this fight with my life. But that was ok.

I looked around at everyone in the brothel that I had grown to look at as my family, and decided that I was tired of them all being treated like garbage by the likes of men like the bull. I may lose my life, but I was determined to show all of them that there were consequences for harming the weak.

Right before I went in to strike, I felt a hand upon my shoulder. The hand was cold as steel and sent a shiver through my body as its fingers dug into my shoulder. The hand was followed by the sound of metal clanking every few seconds. I looked to left and right and saw that the glorious Legionnaires of Britannia had assembled around me with their swords drawn. The one with his hand my shoulder stepped forward and impaled his blade in the wooden floor. Just as the stories had told, his voice boomed as he spoke, "I Sir Merlin of Albion proclaim all those with their swords drawn are hereby under arrest for disrupting the peace of this establishment and attacking innocent civilians. Now you can either come quietly or face the legends that you have no doubt heard so much of."

All was quiet within the brothel as the men backed off slowly, but that soon changed as one imbecile decided to test the legends he had heard for himself. He charged forth and was soon followed by all of his other friends as they all rushed to their certain doom. Despite how much I would have loved to fight alongside such legends, I knew that I had to ensure that everyone was kept out of this scuffle. I took Luciana's hand and motioned all of the other entertainers and servers to retreat to the *Siren's Nest*. We had all prepared for this kind of scenario where a brawl would break out, and so they all allowed themselves to be herded downstairs with relative ease.

The reverberation of blades could be clearly heard ongoing above us as the girls huddled together within the various rooms. I counted the heads and saw that all the girls were accounted for and then went on to find my mother. She was in her own room with Luciana tending to the bruise on her face she received for me. My pace slowed down as I walked to them because I didn't know what to expect from the two of them. Mother saw me approaching and welcomed me with a smile right before she slapped me. Her face was stern like an older woman's but even with that look she began to laugh at me, "I hope that you're proud of yourself Lancelot. You are now the hero you always wanted to be. I wonder how many good men are going to die up there because you couldn't suppress your urge to be a hero, or did you just want to leave so badly that it was worth a few lives?"

Again, it happened again. No matter what the reason was for a fight between me and one of those worthless patrons, she always took their side. At first I had thought, she was right and I was nothing but a problem child when it came to the fights I found myself in, but this time was different. All I had to do to convince myself what I did was right was to look at Luciana's face. I was fully ready to accept my punishment, but I would never allow someone else to pay for the sins that I made.

I was tired. I was so tired of having to deal with this. My frustration was mounting to the degree where my fingers where clutching all of the hairs on my head between them. In a sudden outburst I screamed, "Why, why Mother do you support those vagabonds that look at you as nothing but a piece of trash. I'm the only one that truly loves you here and yet I 'm the one scorned here. No, I'm not the one you're mad at. You're mad at yourself for being so weak and succumbing to your desires to lay with that man. It must kill you to look at me and be reminded of the mistake you made.

My rant was cut short as Luciana's hand now made contact with my face. It was instinct; it was nothing but pure basic instinct that made me react that way. The moment her hand touched my face I swiped away her hand and back handed her myself. I didn't need for her to hit the ground to know what I had done was evil; I didn't need to hear her cry as my hand struck her; I didn't need to see the look in her eyes. I ran the moment I hit her for I knew that I was now no better than the vagabonds I held with such little respect.

    I didn't know where my feet were taking me. My eyes shut themselves as I ran, and ran until a powerful arm wrapped itself around my waist as if it were a snake crushing its prey. My movements ceased as I turned and looked at the blood stained knight that had placed his hand on my shoulder. I took a look around where I was and saw that the brawl was over and surprisingly not a single life had been taken. The ruffians as well as the Legionnaires had their fair share of injuries but nothing fatal. It was an astonishing sight to behold. In order to subdue people such as that lot of ruffians without killing a single one took far more skill than it would have taken to just cut them down.

    The ruffians were being tied up and led outside by several of the Legionnaires that were in the scuffle. My attention turned back to the man that had stopped me. Though he dawned armor of a simple Legionnaire, I could feel that he was much greater than the men he led. He rubbed my hair and bent to one knee so that we were at eye level. Underneath his long white beard was a warm smile that welcomed me. His warm smile further comforted me as he said, "Willing to sacrifice yourself for a loved one is a noble trait that is rarely seen these days. I could tell that before you protected your friend that you were willing to submit to that man Isaac even though you could take him."

I thanked God for finally sending me a soul that understood the actions that I took. But that despite his words I knew that the actions I had taken had ramifications for everyone unless I left *The Lady of Lake*. I removed his hand from me and replied, "Well that makes one person who appreciated it." I tried to continue walking, but the old man grabbed my arm.

"I take it that you're leaving after this incident. I'm sure that Julian would have your head once he learned of what you started."

"Good thing me and my head will be long gone by the time that happens. I thank you for your help good knight. I may not still be standing here if it weren't for your kindness."

"I acted not out of kindness but out of duty lad. Ever since Uther slayed the dragon rampaging our lands and united the lands of Albion, we Britannia Legionnaires decided to live our lives to ensure the safety of our countrymen. That even includes those men over there. While they certainly lack proper etiquette, they are no less men just as we are. We all have our demons and so what right do I have to take the life of a cherished countryman for his demons getting the best of him."

His words touched me as I had come to see my own demons as of late.

"Well whether out of kindness or duty you still have my thanks for your prompt action in this affair."

"It was an honor and give me no thanks because you have aided me in my search a great bit. So the debt has already been paid in full."

"Search? Is this by King Uther's request?"

"No, this is a quest of my own for a student to pass on my knowledge to, and I believe that my search has finally yielded some worthwhile results. I shall be blunt from here on out. I want you to be my new apprentice so gather your things lad and meet and my men outside. The world is a dangerous for a boy your age to travel alone, so it would be in your best interest to accept my offer lad."

Without a chance to even refuse his offer, the old man left me alone in the middle of the tavern. I didn't even need to second guess myself though. This was the chance I had always dreamed of and God had been kind enough to grant me my greatest wish.

I was nothing but a young boy of merely thirteen, so the delusions of freedom that haunted me never had taken full root. I yearned to escape that prison island for so many years, but I could never think to part with Mother nor Luciana. Such convictions crumbled in my hand like a leaf being grinded down to pieces. I quickly ran upstairs while nearly tripping over Roland who seemed to have been greatly injured during the skirmish, but I was nimble enough to regain my balance and keep moving up the stairs. I entered my room with a sense of joy and purpose that had long been lost to me as I spent my life wiping tables and collecting blood money for women like mother. I naively thought that such things would be a lost memory to be as I quickly grabbed my Gladius and took a long look at the remainder of my blades. A fine collection they were, but they would prove useless to me in the trials ahead and oh how I abhorred useless items in my life.

On my way out of the room though I was stopped by the unwelcome sight of Luciana's bruised face. Each side of her cheek was a different shade with the cheek I hit being a purplish tint resembling the base of a rotting tree. I turned my head away from the side and tried to push my way past her, but she gave me no path to take. Her eyes tried to catch mine as a fox does a bouncing rabbit in the meadows, but I did not have the patience of such a creature and decided to look her in the eye as I asked her to move.

Her will with me was just as resolute as with Isaac as she held her ground refusing to give me passage. For a moment, I felt the anger rising in my fist once more, but the mark upon her face cooled my temper as I calmly asked her to move again.

This time she responded to my plea, "Why should I move and allow you to leave me just as my parents once did? Do you think to run away from this mark you gave me Lancelot, if so you are truly a coward."

"Call me what you will Lucy, but I have had it with this place. And remember both you and my mother rejected me so I won't even be all that missed in the end. Now excuse me while I go make a meaning for my life."

My cold words were the perfect key to open the passage she had previously blocked, but even after I passed her she managed to hang onto me slightly to get me to turn around once more.

"You're a fool Lancelot if you thought I rejected your love. Its…just not something I can take where I'm destined to go."

"Funny, at least we both can agree on that sentiment because neither can I."

"Is this how you intend for things to end with everyone Lancelot? Do you intend to just vanish in the night never to return as your father did?"

"Don't ever speak of that man to me! He left for himself. I'm leaving because I never want to hurt you all again. It's better this way. You shall see."

"No blow you could inflict me with would ever cause the same pain of you leaving. This bruise will heal in time, but I fear if I lose you that wound would never recover. Despite what I said, it was the fact that I knew you would be there for me that gave me the strength to get through this life, but without you here…"

My words were the rash one of a boy that knew not how to just simply let go of things. I took her within my arms and felt her tears roll down my arm.

"Then you should come with me. I'm sure there would be no objection…"

Luciana's strength was something that I was never able to truly appreciate until much later in my years, but she broke away from me and wiped the tears from her eyes.

"No, I cannot. If you and I were to leave, then who would look after Vivian. She would be heartbroken to lose the two of us, so I will stay. This is my place."

"No, your place is by me and so I promise you I shall return here one day with the name of Legionnaire and take you and Mother from this life. This I solemnly swear to you my love."

"Yes, just remember that no matter where you go and no matter how much you loathe this place. This lake is your home where you will be always welcome.

We shared one last kiss before my departure and to this day my lips still can feel the tingle of her lips parting from mine. Her smiling face was the last thing I remember of my childhood on that Isle. In no more than just a couple of minutes afterward, I met the old knight by the shore of the lake as he and his men loaded onto their ferry. He took a long look at the only possession I had brought with me that trip: the first blade that had started my collection. I bent to one knee as I had heard was customary for an apprentice to do and planted my short sword in the ground.

"I ready to serve you Sir…"

"Merlin and simply Merlin will do lad. Tell me what your name is lad and where you hail from?"

"Lancelot Sire, Lancelot of the Lake"

## Chapter Three
# Homecoming

**WHEN I WAS** younger, the strain of rowing the oars all the way across the lake was too much for me. It was because of this that I could never leave the island without the aid of Roland or one of the other guys there. It was relieving to be able to make the journey from the mainland to the middle of the lake with no one's help. As the bow of the canoe grounded on the shore, I leapt from the seat to the shoreline and ran my fingers through the sand. The grains slipped through my fingers just as freely as they always had.

Three years. I had been free from this place for only three years and yet my soul still beckoned me to return to this place the moment Merlin allowed me a couple days to myself. I stood on the edge of the water as I looked into the dark depths to only see myself peering right back at me. I remembered that before I left, I looked into this very same water and saw a straggly boy running away from his old life to capture his dream of freedom.

That naïve boy was dead now.

And in his place was a lean man who devoted himself

to eradicating any that stained the name of Albion through his selfish actions. I may have been guided by the laws set forth by Uther Pendragon, but I served no man but myself. A nearby frog leapt into my reflection and made the image dissolve leaving nothing but the shine of the moon upon the surface of the water. Just as the ripples from the frog's impact hit my feet, I turned around and proceeded up the hill to *The Lady of the Lake*. Even before I entered the building, I could tell that some improvements had been made since my departure. Waiting at the door to greet me was a woman I had never seen before with a golden smile that was sure to entice any man. She wrapped her arm within mine and began running her mouth about only God knows what. Normally I always would lend my ear to any lady regardless of class, but I was on a mission that night and I had no time to deal with her rants about the great pricing options available for me if I decided to rent a room (another new feature no doubt).

My eyes couldn't believe themselves as we walked through the door. The quaint tavern that I had served in as a boy had been transformed into more of a whorehouse. Red exotic drapes hung from the ceiling that complemented the crimson dresses of the dancers performing to the music in the back. The creaky wooden floor had been replaced with a new freshly coated wooden floor. There were twice as many candles that illuminated the room resulting in flickering shadows dancing across the walls. I broke off from my guide and took a seat at one of the empty tables. Perhaps only a moment after I had taken a seat, a young boy probably twelve years of age came to my table with feather and paper in hand. His clothes were worn down to the point where I was confident that he had worn that same outfit day after day in his entire life. His hair was a tangled mess which was most likely thanks in part to him not having any parents. I had seen many children like him over the last few years.

It unfortunately was a common sight in these changing times. Ever since the Romans pulled the majority of their forces from Britannia, we as a people have suffered greatly for it. I was not the only child to have been fathered by Roman soldier who was abandoned when recalled to his homeland. It was a tale that had become common place for many children. The true tragedy though was that the mothers of these children were often slaves that were given to these officers as entertainment to ensure an officer wouldn't go have his way with any random peasant girl that he ran into. The children of these relationships were often discarded as unnecessary baggage.

These thoughts lingered within me as I looked upon the destitute state the child was obviously in. I asked for nothing but a mug of ale and gave the kid an extra gold coin to help him get by. I was sure that he would no doubt spend on something frivolous or even just have it stolen from him.

As he walked away, I could see through one of the tears in his ragged tunic that there were several bruises all over his back. His body frame was on the wiry side of things, so it was entirely possible that he managed to spill quite a few orders which would no doubt in turn lead to a few bruises from the locals. When I was younger, I had foolishly believed that me standing up to those ruffians would have inspired others to take a stand or to make them naturally stop oppressing the servers. Those were nothing but the dreams of a boy that had been secluded on an island. The world is just as Mother had said it was. Only the shine of coins and the cold touch of steel could change the world around us. That was the world's one and only truth.

My ale came to me in a prompt manner but served this time by a beautiful woman who no doubt had to be Aula, an entertainer that had been coming into her own role around the time of my departure. She and I had never gotten to know one another well so it was no surprise that she seemed to not recognize me. Then again I was no longer like the boy that had just served me who barely had any suitable rags to wear. I had strolled in *The Lady of the Lake* wearing a black, leather short sleeved tunic coupled with a matching pair of black trousers and topped off with leather sandals. It was a sporting outfit that had allowed me to catch a fair share of looks from men and women alike as I entered.

The one to have taken the highest interest in my attire was Aula. Her hands caressed my shoulders as she walked away hoping no doubt I would pay for her services. I glanced back and threw a smile her way as I dutifully watched her hips swing when she walked. She was good. Not nearly as good as Mother, but she had a certain charm to her that I certainly found myself enjoying. Despite how nice it was to see a somewhat familiar face, she was not the woman I had hoped would approach me. I scanned the entire room and saw no sign of Luciana, a fact that made me quickly finish off the rest of my drink and then order another. I suppose that there was still a bit of that foolish naiveté in me that had hoped she would have remained a serving wench. The fact that I didn't see her roaming the tavern section was a clear indication that she was most likely entertaining a patron.

While I scanned the room, one thing in particular did manage to put a smile on my face. Gambling in a game of dice in the corner was none other than Isaac, the bull. He had not changed at all over the years. Well aside from the fact that he only had one hand now for some peculiar reason. As he rolled a pair of die, I could hear his roar of frustration all the way from where I was sitting. He was losing no doubt. I figured that I had a couple of minutes to spare before I had to continue on my mission, so I stopped by his table and joined him and his friends in a game of dice. From the look on their faces, I could see that they had been there for quite some time drinking. Their heads swayed back and forth as their speech slurred with what was either an invite to play or an insult. I couldn't really determine which one. I picked up a couple of die and rolled them casually to see that lady luck was with me that night. Without a word said between us, well a coherent word I mean, I left their table after taking my earnings and sought out Aula.

She was flaunting her goods over by another table when I came from behind her and sprinkled the ten gold coins I had earned from that game down her gown. She immediately stopped what she was doing and grabbed my hand as she took me to *The Siren's Nest*.

As we worked our way through the tavern, she decided to ask me a little about myself. She pressed herself against my side and asked, "So handsome, it's not every day that a fellow like you strolls into a place like this. I nearly had to fight off all the other girls to call dibs on you and that long raven hair of yours."

Complimenting my hair was a nice touch. She had obviously become quite skilled over the years, but if you asked me with a face like hers the last thing she needed to use were words. I found myself laughing at the idea that women that had raised me now fought over who would lay with me. It was a peculiar notion to say the least, but growing up in places such as *The Lady of the Lake* had a way of making a man take such statements as nothing more than a mere compliment. I flashed her another smile as we continued down the stairs and I said, "Good thing that you won out then. I happen to have a habit of only going for the best and I like what I see so far."

She blushed as she led me into her room. Before I followed her in, I paused at the door and ran my hand across a pair of notches that had been made along the right side of it. The notches ran all the way up to my chest and crudely initialed next to them were the letters L.L.

Lancelot and Luciana. I had almost forgotten how the two of us would always mark how big we had gotten every year on that door. I smiled how my notch was consistently higher than hers. Despite her age, I had always proven to be taller than her. It was a fact that she despised. I pulled out one of my daggers and added another notch in the wall that towered over my previous mark I made not too long before I had left. With that done, I proceeded into Aula's room and closed the door behind me.

That night went like many other nights I had experienced

beforehand with ladies such as her. I became lost within a sea of passion between the two of us. When I was under those sheets, I forgot who I was and who I was aspiring to be. The only thing that mattered was moment, and I ensured that the moment lasted for quite some time. The idea of that act being a special one had long since passed and had been replaced with the fact that I was just acting out of pure instinct and satisfaction. When I left, her panting only helped illuminate the smile she tried her best to hide. Entertainers such as her prided themselves on the fact that they pleasured the patrons not the patrons pleasuring them. I'm sure that she soon realized that there were those that shattered that philosophy.

    I closed the door and walked towards the end of the hallway to another door where the name Vivian had been carved deeply and elegantly into the wood. The memories surrounding my last visit to Mother's room were still as fresh as ever within my mind. My hand still tingled with unprecedented shame as I thought back to striking Luciana. I was thankful that I had taken that detour to Aula's room because she had helped me work off a good deal of stress as I approached this moment, the reason for my return there. I knocked twice on her door and waited for her to open it. For a long while, I stood there in silence without hearing a sound. I knocked twice on the door once more and still no answer. Mother had always answered the door in the past even if she was with a client. I couldn't imagine why in the world she neglected to answer it now. I feared the worse as if perhaps she simply couldn't answer it due to some scoundrel holding her against her will. The simple idea had taken full root within my mind as I drew my precious Roman short sword which I now called *Fang*. With one powerful charge, I rammed my shoulder into the door and burst into the room ready to take as many heads as need be. My eagerness quickly diminished as I saw a fat man of epic proportions on top of Mother. With a girl like squeal, the man hurried out of the room while covering his private parts. I could only imagine the laughs that would occur upstairs as he jiggled through the brothel.

It didn't take me long to figure out what I fool I was and my face began to redden as Mother, who was frightened as well by this armed stranger, took a closer look at me. The bed sheets that she was covering herself with fell to the ground as she rushed toward me and held me in her arms. I was reluctant at first to hold her considering how our last encounter had went, but soon those thoughts left my mind as my arms took hold of her tightly and I rested my head upon her dainty shoulder. She took a step back and smiled as she sized me up. Her hand caressed my cheek as a proud smile emerged on her face.

"My son", she said. "My precious, precious boy. My look how you've grown and your hair is so long now. It's all so different. I could scarcely recognize you for a moment Lancelot."

That smile of hers. It had been the focal point of many dreams in my life. Despite the life Mother had been forced to give me, I never held any malice or ill will towards her in any way. In all honesty, I found it almost unbearable to be separated from the woman that nurtured me for so long as I traveled with Merlin. I saw many things that reminded me of her from the endless grassy meadows that showed her boundless love for me. The setting sun as it cast its crimson glow over the horizon reminded me of her smooth skin. No matter where I went I found myself missing her at every turn, but now I had returned and I intended to right the wrong I made so long ago. We went to her bed and I laid my head down on her lap as she stroked my hair just as she did when I was a boy. Her perfume still floated around her giving her such a pleasant smell that reminded me of the many nights as a child I just wanted to nuzzle my face between her bosom. As she continued to stroke my hair, she laughed when she found a long strand of Aula's hair on my shoulder. She dangled it in front of me with playful smile on her face, "So I see that you had yourself a little fun before you came to see me."

I smiled proudly as I took the strand of hair from her and tossed it aside. I replied to her, "It was not my initial idea Mother, but it was just too good of an opportunity to turn down."

"I suppose it's only natural that you would want to lay with one of the women that nurtured you since you were a child. Seeing them prance around naked pleasuring our patrons must have had an interesting effect on you growing up. Didn't you find it strange when you took her in your arms?"

"Strange…no. I have never found the act to be strange. I have actually found the act to be very enjoyable like taking a stroll by the lake side. It doesn't matter who you take the walk with because the scenery and the experience will be the same."

"I see, so that's how you view it now. What a complete turnaround from the boy that declared his love to a girl after one night."

"I was nothing but a boy then Mother. I based my feelings on nothing but a passionate moment which was a mistake. Luciana is very dear to me indeed, but I realize that I should not have lain with her. Since I've left, I have been with many women and none of them made me feel like Luciana did."

Mother gently pushed my head off of her lap and then walked toward her armoire. For a couple of moments, she muttered what I had said again and again until she began to laugh the same way she did that day three years ago.

"I see that you really have grown up to see the world for what it is Lancelot. It's such a shame that Luciana didn't have your mindset after you left."

I nearly fell off the edge of her bed once I heard her name. The way she had said those words were perhaps the coldest I have heard her voice be. The room became very quiet until I heard myself yelling at her in a sudden rage.

"What do you mean…What happened to Luciana Mother!"

She turned back towards me and brandished one of her classic masks that she wore on her face while dealing with her clients. Her eyes began to water as she tried to speak but her voice continued to get choked up. I had seen her use this method many times in the past, so the fact that she believed she could use that one me was preposterous.

"Lancelot…I'm so sorry to have to tell you this but Luciana is no longer here and hasn't been for the past two years."

My voice was stern as I stared her mask down showing no signs of being taken in by her ploy. I had no idea what had happened to her, but I knew that Mother was somehow in the thick of it and possessed none of the sorrow she exuded.

"What happened to her Mother?"

"I knew that you two cared for one another, but I never expected for her to take such rash actions for you. Look I understand why you thought you had to leave, but that broke her heart. She didn't eat for days and refused to see anyone but worse of all she refused to work and as you know her line of work had just recently changed."

Not eating? There's no way that could have been right. It was true that Luciana was a dependent girl, but it wasn't to the degree of if I left she would have shut down like that. Mother had to be lying to me, but then again maybe it wasn't such a stretch for her to shut down like that. Despite whatever she said, having to look forward to a life of being nothing more than tool for patrons to do with as they pleased was a perhaps too much for her to handle.

"Mother, you helped her right. You were able to talk some sense into her right! Right!"

"I tried my best darling, but you had really put a spell over her. Maybe she always had but after you left she became enamored with you. The idea of another man that wasn't you touching her brought her to tears every time. No matter who I brought in to comfort her and show her the error of such dangerous thoughts she would send them all away. She told me she just wanted to wait for you to come back and she would never sell herself for a man less than you."

The fool. That foolish girl. After all of those years of saying the games we played with one another meant nothing, she went and succumbed to the passionate night we had. While the idea of her caring so much was an endearing one that brought me joy it also brought my heart nothing but pity and sadness. I didn't need to have Mother tell me the rest of the story because I knew how this would end. She undoubtedly left two years ago never to return most likely while in search of me. I wish that was how it turned out indeed. I quickly got up and walked toward the door only to have Mother grab my arm to halt my movement.

She spun me around to face her eye to eye and continued telling her story, "Lancelot, she didn't leave the brothel by her own will. Lord Julian sold her to a band of Saxon mercs for around a hundred pieces of gold."

The news hit me harder than I would have anticipated it to. Never in all my life would I have expected to hear Luciana had been sold off as she was nothing but an article of clothing. I jerked my hand away from Mother and leaned against the wall for a moment. Luciana, my best friend and first love had been sold off. My hair dangled in front of my eyes as I looked at the floor. The Saxons were a group of nomadic warriors from the mainland that were giving the Romans a good deal of trouble on many of their borders. During this conflict, a good deal of their people have come here as well operating as mercs or raiders. They were a barbaric group that showed no mercy to any of their victims whether woman or child and the thought of poor Lucy being in their clutches was too much to bear.

"How could you let him sell her off like that! She was like a daughter to you! Where is your shame?"

"Don't you dare try to lecture me on shame and honor when last time I checked you ran away from here with your tail between your legs like a dog that had done something wrong. I tried my best to help Luciana for a long time while all you did was go off playing soldier with for that landless King Uther."

"Playing soldier? I was off making something of the boy that you so dutifully raised in a brothel devoid of morals and laws. The Legionnaires may not be as heroic as I once thought, but at least they stand for something in these times unlike you Mother. All you stand for is how low citizens must fall in order to make a life for themselves."

"Well you fit in perfectly with that bunch who solely care for the orders their fat king barks out. Well while you are making something of yourself out there, girls like Luciana are being sold like cattle. Is this the land that you pride yourself in fighting for? You may hate the life I live by, but on this island where the only law is that of Lord Julian's I have done much more for you than any King and yet I am the villain. Besides if there is anyone to blame you should place the sword at your own two feet."

"What does that mean Mother?"

"Luciana's defiance was a well-guarded among the entertainers here for a good year. Lord Julian was none the wiser until things began to slowly unravel with the arrival of that one Legionnaire. He came alone one night already in a half drunken stupor claiming that he knew you. Once your name had been uttered from his mouth, even I flocked to him to listen to him recount your tales since you departed. While we all expected to hear tales of your courage in training, we instead heard how you were a great warrior between the sheets of nearly every young girl you came across village to village. His words continue to destroy Luciana as she saw him produce a necklace that he claimed to won from you in a game of dice. The necklace, the only memento from her mother, was the very same one she gave to you when you first left. Seeing it in the hands of another sent her into a blind rage, as she went about cursing your name and running out of the place. I had figured she would return once she had calmed down but two full weeks went by until Lord Julian himself came by with her bound to prevent her escape again. It was not long after that she was sold off."

The necklace, I indeed had forgotten the origins of the trinket until Mother reminded me. It was a gift that Luciana gave me before I left as a promise that I would always love her and soon return. I was in such a hurry to leave that it seemed like a trifle thing I never paid too much attention to until that game of dice. Still, I blamed Mother for allowing her to run in the first place.

"You failed to act upon your oath as a mother to her and allowed her to run away, but now I'll act upon the one I made when I became Merlin's apprentice, to seek out truthful justice for the land. I will find Luciana at any cost so that she knows she can at least depend on one person she thought cared for her."

I left Mother once again without another word said and dragged my feet through the brothel until I made it to the shore of the lake once more. I had no desire to stay in that place any longer, so I slept alone for the first time in a while in that canoe looking out at the twinkling stars.

As I awoke, the Sun shined with a radiant brilliance that would have made me gaze up at the sky in wonder and awe, but not that day. Despite how brilliantly it shined, the world around me was a dark one. It was in this darkness that I was able to set out on the path that would define me as a man but it was this same path that would first destroy the man I wanted to be.

Waiting at the shore for me was Merlin along with a couple other Legionaries who by the look of their faces have had a fair amount of adventures on the island recently while I slept in the canoe. I looked at Merlin with his pale grayish eyes and I bent to one knee once more as I had done three years ago. I drew *Fang* and laid it at the feet of my master before I made my request, "Merlin, there has been a kidnapping of a fair maiden by the like of a group of Saxon mercs. I will not lie and say that I do not know of this woman. She was a dear friend to me master and I wish to liberate her from her bonds of imprisonment to those barbarians. I know we took an oath not to get involved with the affairs of the Saxons, but I need to save her Master."

Merlin was silent but his gaze was definitive. I knew I would receive no aid from him for he would never father the idea of betraying the law of Uther. I was ready to leave it at that until Dalton began to run his mouth saying, "Leave to the son of a whore to try to break the creed established by Uther. We were told not to harm the Saxons in exchange for them raiding Pict villages north of Hadrian's Wall."

Dalton…I already knew that he was the one to have told Luciana of my various activities and broke her heart, so he was just as much to blame as Mother was. He and I had never found common ground aside for our mutual hatred.

I knew he would mock my request, so I held no grudge

at the time as I simply just walked along the shore to my canoe. But he soon gave me all the reason I needed to hate him even further. As he shouted out towards me, "By the way Lancelot, your mother is an animal I can see where you get your talents from."

    I barely gave him enough time to even laugh for long as he soon found a throwing knife lodged deep in his neck. Blood gushed forward from his final laughs as he fell to the ground. I knew not if Merlin and his men gave chance because I was soon on my way to my canoe and began rowing towards the shore as a newly branded outlaw of Albion.

*Chapter Four*
# Galahad

**HER FINGERS SLID** across my back as she woke me up with a gentle kiss. Lying before my eyes was a pale skinned beauty with her exotic black hair covering her face completely. I reached to part her hair but the moment my fingers grazed it I was jerked back to reality. I woke up for real at that moment to see that it was just Elaine sharing the bed with me still. I left her side and walked towards the window and took in a breath of fresh air that eased my nerves. Dawn was still settling in upon the village as I retrieved my clothes to venture outside and take in the climbing sunrise. I crept outside the house as quietly as possible so to not wake her and grabbed my leather skin canteen and headed to the well. As I left the house, I was not the only villager of Dale to have gotten the idea to fetch the morning's first bucket of water. Already tugging at the rope with his small blistered hands was Galahad, Elaine's son. I snuck up behind the kid and quickly picked him up right as he had managed to pull a bucket just brimming with water. His high pitched giggle made me smile as I spun him around a few times before placing him back on his feat.

The water looked pristine as I used it to fill my canteen and then take Galahad's hand in mine and escort him back home. His hand gripped onto mine tightly as he shined a silly smile towards me. It amazed me how he could smile such a smile full with such innocence and happiness in these times. While the Kingdom of Cornwall had been barely scathed by Roman occupation of the last few centuries, they were still going through turmoil of their own in these changing times. King Mark's rule, was one full of discord as he struggled to assimilate the former regions that were controlled by his brothers into his own. Officially the entirety of the Kingdom belonged to him by birthright, but rumors of foul play and honorless tactics to remove his brothers from power lingered in the air which ignited much resistance to his take over. To further add to their troubles, the people of Cornwall were just as heavily victimized by the recent attacks from the Picts and like the rest of Britannia. Due to the ridiculous infighting going on, the King and his men did not have the man power yet to be able to safeguard the villages against the frequent raids that occurred against them. The common ideal that had been adopted by many of the villages throughout all of Britannia was that we were on our own from both the Romans and our Kings. With that mindset in place, it was hard for the children to truly live the free spirited lives they were supposed to. Many of them were off plowing the fields with their fathers or tending to the livestock. Galahad had been no exception to this and yet he still continued to smile. I wish that I had his innocence when I was his age.

The journey back to his home was a short one as we spent our time racing to see which one between the two of us could catch the most leaves before they landed on the ground. Though I knew I looked ridiculous in doing such a game, it had become a habit of ours since I first met him when he was five. I took a good look at him as he pranced around flaying his arms about reaching for the seasoned leaves of autumn. It had been four years since I met him. In fact he and his mother, Elaine, were among the first people I had met when I left with Merlin. Back then, the child was a mere shell of how he was now. I can still remember how fragile he looked as he lay on his sick bed, but now he was a boy quickly growing into a man. There was little doubt in my mind that he would end up bigger than me as well.

When we returned back to his home, we were greeted by a wonderful smell that had both of us running into the house. Elaine had made a full spread for us that morning and we wasted no time jumping right into the feast laid out before us. That was how many mornings had been the past year that I stayed with the two of them. At first the idea of living a normal life terrified me, but I had grown to actually enjoy the life of a simple villager to a strong degree. The work I did every morning for them on their farm was honest work that made me feel that I was actually helping somehow enjoy themselves for more than just minutes like my previous occupation had dealt with. The scenery of the country was majestic along with the peace that accompanied it, and the best part was being able to return every night after I was done training to a woman who was dedicated to helping me find Luciana.

Galahad quickly put the finishing touches on his breakfast as he said his goodbyes and went out to play with the other children of Dale. Since I arrived, at my behest, the villagers allow their children to gather in the village square and play before they have to begin their work for the day. I just couldn't stand the idea of children being forced to work like dogs.

As customary after a meal, I cleaned the plates for Elaine while she just watched me. It was a certainly uncomfortable habit that she possessed but as long as she provided me with meal and boarding then I had no right to complain. Once I was sure Galahad was gone, I asked Elaine, "How much longer do you think it will be?"

She came behind me and tugged at my shirt a little as her other fingers played with my hair and said, "I don't know Lancelot. According to my information, they will arrive here sometime soon in order to restock on supplies before they head back to wherever their base camp is."

"You've been saying that for months Elaine. If I have to wait any longer, then I'm sure to lose my mind."

"Oh, I'm not so sure about that. And don't forget after your little stunt you are a wanted man. It was for your best interest to lay low for a year so they would lose interest in you. I can see that the process is wearing on you now, but despite your urgent need to save this girl, you love it here. You can try to put on a mask around me to hide your true feelings, but I can see your true face when you deal with Galahad. You treat the child as your own son."

She spoke nothing but the truth there. I had begun to enjoy my time there, but at the end of the day I knew where my heart truly was. I had to find Luciana at any cost.

"He is a cute kid that is oblivious to the life that surrounds him. It's natural that I exude a nice demeanor around him to ensure he remains that way. The world is a dark place where the only light is the shine of a coin. It's a harsh truth, but one I'd prefer he knew very little of."

"Again with your Mother's golden saying huh. Lancelot dear, you need to take a more positive outlook to life."

"The fact that my mother was an entertainer molded who I am today and I have no shame in that. Besides I find it ironic that I'm being lectured on how money doesn't bring happiness by someone who is a spy for Rome."

"*Was* a spy for Rome. I now like to consider myself an informant for anyone with enough coin or comeliness in your case."

"Well I just hope that my nightly payments bring about the results that I desire soon"

"Relax love, I have never failed when it came to a job Lancelot especially if I am well paid for it, and you Sir have indeed paid me quite well."

She gave me a sly smile as she left the room and I wondered how such a pure and innocent child like Galahad came from such a woman like Elaine. Ever since the first day I laid my eyes upon her, I knew she was not to be trusted, but Merlin said she had been a valuable asset for Rome and now she worked for King Uther to keep an eye on King Mark's activities.

Since I left home, Merlin had taught me much about the ways of the Legionaries along with the ways of the sword, but when it came to the world around me I was as fresh as a new born babe. I had no idea of how society worked for the most part. Everything thing I knew, I had acquired due to my time at the brothel and there were very few life skills that were harped on there. I had no sense of common courtesy, etiquette, or how to carry myself in public. For some time, Merlin tried his best to instill these values in me himself, but he too had a very dismal background as he had always lived by the sword, so he knew and I knew that he would prove to be a poor teacher. Merlin made sure that Elaine would instill all of those lessons into me along with many more. She was a renowned information broker that had a knack for getting her info through questionable means. She was a woman surrounded in mystery and Mother had always warned me those were the ones you always tried your best to avoid.

    I was left with her for five months and during that time I learned all there was to know about the world. Her lessons were not the type I could define as being taught with tender instruction. She believed in hands on experience in order to grow and thus she led me into one incommodious situation after another. It was under her harsh tutelage that I learned how to read and write, skills that had not seemed that crucial to possess until she broke it down for me. And under her care I learned not to fight with my blade but rather to fight with words and how the clothes I wore didn't define me but the faces I wore. While a sword could easily keep you alive in a fight, I found that words and smiles can avoid a fight entirely and get even more than the desired results.

    Her training methods aside, I should be grateful though for people like her because if not for her I would have most likely perished by then looking for Luciana and getting into a fight with more than a dozen Saxon raiders or something. As it turns out, Luciana had been seen traveling with a group of mercs known as the Free Riders. While it was rare to witness a group of mercs working with each other, the problems faced by the people of Britannia made such a rarity a common occurrence. For the last six years after the Romans pulled off, we have been left to fend for ourselves, a notion that was foreign for the majority of the people. They had lived their lives as farmers and their father had been a farmer and so their children were raised as farmers. None of them knew the first thing about a sword, but instead of banding together and learning how to deal with our own problems we asked for outside aid in the form of countless Saxon mercenary bands in order to fight off the occasional attack from the Picts and from the North.

Because of our weakness, the common folk have seen these mercs as a sort of protector and thus they were always more than eager to shower them with gifts whenever a mercenary band rolled through a village. Elaine had mention for quite some time that the group that bought Luciana was to come through Dale for supplies soon and when they arrived I had every intention of taking her back one way or another. Unfortunately, I had not made much progress on my actual plan of action regarding how to rescue her. Originally I had hoped that Merlin and the other Legionaries would assist me in any plan that I had in mind, but such assistance would go against the creed that they lived by.

When King Uther came into power, one of the first things that he implemented was assembling all of the greatest warriors still left in Albion, the chieftains of various tribes, and former Roman soldiers and gave them the official title of Legionnaire. It was a symbol of greatness among the newly assembled soldiers of Albion , just as the Romans had once done. The Legionnaires served as the elite of Albion's newly formed army, but when given such a lofty title, it is only natural that the members bearing the name looked down upon the requests the villagers made for protection.

Time and time again I have heard the patrons that attended the brothel rave on about how Uther and his men were nothing but a pompous group of Rome lovers that cared nothing for the common folk. When I joined the Legionnaires, I had hoped that those claims were false, but after a couple of years of training to join their ranks I found the rumors were true to a fault. While Merlin proved to be a constant class act, the others that followed him were nothing but the sons of Rome that decided not to return to their homeland or the followers of the four great chieftains, Leodegrance, Merlin, Pelles, and Lot looking to maintain a shred of their former power in this new land. They cared naught for the people of Albion: their only concern was obtaining a high enough status so that they could live comfortably. It was because of that selfish belief that I was not surprised when they refused to aid me in my mission to save Luciana. There would be no profit for any of them. Without an explicit order from King Uther, they would never take any action unless they were caught in the cross fire of an attack like that time at the brothel. Such arrogance! What gave them the right to abandon the oaths that they took? When I was a boy, it was my dream to be just like one of them, but just like any other things in life age has a fine way of corroding our childish naiveté.

I scraped off the last bit of food from the plate and marveled at my work. After carefully stacking the plates, I went outside to check in Galahad. Per usual, instead of playingvwith the other children during this time, he was hard at work swinging my blade, *Fang*. The boy had always taken a liking to swordsmanship and whenever he got the chance I could find him practicing with my blade. I came up from behind him and grabbed his wrist right as he was in the middle of a back swing my way. Once he saw me behind him, he quickly dropped my blade and went down to his knees apologizing. Whether he was sorry for almost cutting me or the fact he took my blade once again without permission mattered naught to me. I rubbed my fingers against one another and smiled as the sweat from Galahad's wrist made them slide smoothly across my hand. The kid had been hard at work for sure and I figured I should reward him for his diligence.

I removed my shirt and tossed him one of my twin daggers that I dubbed with the name of *Vivian* and *Luciana*. He fumbled around trying to get a grasp of *Vivian* in his hand and right as he did he looked up to see me bearing down upon him with my blade. With a stunning display of pure instinct, he clumsily rolled out of the way and avoided my strike. Though he didn't have the most graceful movements, the kid had a natural feel to the environment around himself: a vital aspect when it came to fighting. I motioned him to attack me and with no hesitation he charged at me thrusting my dagger at me. I easily deflected the attack and disarmed him because of the force I deflected the dagger with. As Galahad shook his wrist in pain, I kicked him the dagger and began to chastise him, "Galahad! A pure thrust is the simplest attack to either evade or counter. Those kinds of attacks should only be used as a counter to a parry or whilst you have your enemy caught off guard. Now come at me once more."

The kid had a competitive fire that drove him. He took up the dagger once more and attacked. Again and again I deflected his attacks, but he was slowly improving. By the time he was panting on the ground, the sun was already retreating towards its western horizon. Despite how easy he was to fight, I had to admit that he had even worn me down a tad as well. I went over to him and we both took a seat at the base of a tree. The cool bark of the tree felt amazing against my moist backside and coupled along with the shade it provided I was left in a state of tranquility as I watched the leaves dancing in the wind. I reached out for one only to have it flutter away at the touch of my finger tips. I looked over toward Galahad to see that he had a solemn expression plastered on his face. It was truly a rare occasion to see that kid without a smile on his face. I messed up his hair in a futile attempt to make him smile, but all he did was now direct those forlorn eyes my way. I couldn't stand the look in his eyes, so I had no choice but to ask what was bothering him at the moment, "Galahad, what is it that plagues your mind on such a day like today? Surely you are not disheartened by the fact that you couldn't beat me."

His gaze shifted away slightly seemingly out of shame before he responded to my inquiry, "You are just so strong Lancelot. You have the power to do whatever you want and not be bound by the world. I want that strength. I have grown sick of this village and wish to leave and go my own adventures just as you have."

Freedom huh? I suppose that he has reached that age

when he starts to wonder about the world outside his village. There was such a time when I wondered about the very same thing and I convinced Luciana to run away with me that very night. After making it to about the shore of the island, we got cold feet and ran back to the brothel with tears streaming down our faces. I closed my eyes as a cool breeze passed by us and sighed, "Galahad you are but a child. There is no reason for you to rush out into the world so early. There is plenty of time ahead of you. Besides I have no idea where you obtained the delusion that I had been on these extravagant adventures but I can assure you that I have not nor will I do go on some epic quest where the bards will sing of my name for years to come. The strength I have now is all thanks to my days with the Legionnaires and that's all."

"So then you're a Legionnaire like Mother's friend Merlin?"

"God no. I was never cut out to be that kind of person having to blindly obey the commands of a King that is sitting comfortably on his throne whilst I would lay my life on the line for him. I thought I could be one and there was a time where I desired to be one, but I am more suited to be a lone wolf pursuing my own ideals of justice and not adhering to the ones of those who have a better station than me. That way when I die at least I can die by my own terms fighting for what I earnestly believe in.

"And what is it that you believe in?"

"I don't know that answer yet. I believe that I'm still looking for it myself. What I can tell you though Galahad is to fight with everything you have when you find that thing to believe in. That way you will never allow the precious things in your life to slip through your fingers."

Galahad rubbed his fingers together and gave me another innocent smile. My hand reached for his head to rub it once more, but the sound of a jarring fog horn echoing throughout Dale stopped it. My heart stopped when I the sound resonated within my ears. Galahad's eyes and mine met in an instance as he knew exactly what to do next. While it pained me to some degree to rely on a child for assistance in order to save Luciana, I decided long ago that there was no risk too great if it guaranteed her safety. Galahad showed not an ounce of fear as I gave him the signal to approve the actions he would soon take. His hands were steady as he took a firm grip on *Vivian* and raised the blade above his hand.

*Chapter Five*

# Saxon

**THE HORNS CONTINUED** to resonate through the village as I made my way to the village square. It was my first time hearing the fabled horns of the Saxon warriors and they were just as foreboding as I had imagined. The booming sound had a low hollow ring to it that lingered in the air for quite some time until it faded to obscurity. In most occasions, that horn would be bellowed for the sole purpose of signaling an attack against an enemy ship at sea, but here on the mainland it had become a call to any nearby villages that an army for hire was passing through that was willing to do all the tasks that the Kings of Britannia refused to do for their subjects. From simple tasks such as guard duty to the more complex tasks such as bounties, those men handled it all, and if there was one thing that I knew about the village of Dale it was that they had an extensive list of tasks they needed done.

    With sunlight receding from the sky quickly, I knew that I didn't have much time to reach the village before the Saxons decided on a job and then promptly left. The woods were without a sound as I raced through them with nothing but my own pants to be heard. I had been running for quite some time by then and I had become aware of the crimson trail I was leaving behind. The blood trickling from my forehead had blurred my vision leaving my eyes with a stinging sensation coursing through them. After running for around twenty minutes, I could see the villagers through the trees gathering around a caravan loaded with the supplies I had seen the villagers preparing for the Saxons for quite some time as a form of payment for whatever ordeals that they were to take on. My hand pressed against the gash across my face as I tried my best to stop the bleeding. The wound was deeper than I had wanted but the precision of the slash was well placed and ensured that scar would not hamper me in any way. Blood continued to flow out freely despite my measures taken against it which only made me hurry my pace. I was losing more and more blood by the second and if I happened to pass out on my way to the village, then all of my efforts would have been for naught leading up to this point. My injured presence had now caught the attention of the villagers as I jogged into the village.

Despite my year of residency there, I was still known as more of a stranger or some kind of rumor that floated through the town. I made a note to hardly ever be seen by the villagers under the pretext that I was deathly ill to not arouse any suspicions that would attract the Legionnaires there. So the sight of me coming running through the village wounded was perhaps the most exciting thing to occur to them in quite a while. I could hear the hushed murmurs working their way through the crowd until I finally reached the center of the gathering. The gathered crowd was immense and made pushing through their ranks much harder. Their sweaty bodies pressed up against me as I pushed my bloody hand through the crowd. The sight of my crimson stained hand caused them to quickly disperse leaving a clear path to the unit of Saxons that were busy sorting their newly acquired supplies. With one clearly desperate maneuver, I threw myself at the feet of one of the men as I begged him to hear me out, "My son! Please help my son! I'll pay you whatever you desire, but please help me save my son!"

The moment I mentioned the money I had suddenly become worth their attention: typical of the Saxon Mercs. I raised my head and finally got a good look at the band of mercs I had labored for so long to find. I had heard many stories of how these sea born raiders were supposed to look like giant imps brandishing iron weaponry, but the truth was far more disturbing. Because of my position on the ground, the only sight I was able to see for a moment was one of the Saxon's manhood as he proudly wore a rough, leather Rome style tunic only. I quickly rolled away from that man as I tried my best to block the images from my mind.

The man who I presumed to be their leader came before me and spoke in a harsh Germanic tongue that was nearly impossible to discern when I first heard it. I should have not been surprised by obvious differences in our dialect, but my reaction proved otherwise. After hearing his voice, I almost laughed with my first reaction, but due to the pain of the wound I suffered. The laugh came out as more of a squeal that in turn caused the Saxons to erupt with laughter all around me.

While the prospect of them looking down at me, was infuriating I preferred that outcome rather than they knowing how I felt about their ilk. The Saxons were infamous for their quick tempers and how those tempers often led to a display of their prominent skills in battle. From the stories my Mother and Merlin told me, they were a society of hard men that valued strength above all. There was never any room for the weak in their ranks. I have heard a plethora of cruel tales that they do to their young in order to breed them into the sea faring battle lords that mothers tell their children about in their beds. I remember my own Mother lecturing me after I had tried to run away with Luciana that one time years ago about the phantom Saxon pirates that sailed on black summer nights to whisk little boys and girls that had been bad from their bedsides to join their phantom crew for all eternity. After hearing that story, I could not sleep for an entire week without *Fang* in my hand out of pure fear.

Now there I was just a couple of feet from the men that I had once feared so intently as a child with every intention of trying to join their ranks, but in order to do that first I had to sell my story about Galahad. After their laughter had calmed down, I was given the opportunity to state my case once more. I took a good look at how well these men were armed. There were about eight of them in total all dawning light iron greaves and horned helms. Every one of them wielded a crude iron battle axe that any warrior could tell that been worn down by countless battles. When dealing with men such as these, it was the best opportunity to use the new oratory skills that Elaine had imbued upon me.

I felt a hand graze my shoulder and I looked back to find

a tear filled Elaine ready to play her part. She slowly helped me up to my feet and wrapped her hand within mine as we stood before the Free Riders. I stepped forward and tried my best to sound choked up as I spoke saying, "Our son Galahad has been kidnapped by a group of bandits. I tried my best to stop them…but…but I failed him as a father and couldn't do it. So please help me save our son from these outlaws. I'm willing to pay whatever you want for your services."

    I tightened my grip around Elaine's hand as I waited for their reply. I half expected them to at least huddle together and discuss their intentions before they gave n answer, but one of the men who had been resting against the supplies they had gathered got up and stepped towards Elaine and I. His cheeks were flushed telling me that he must be the resident drunk among their outfit and my suspicions were confirmed the moment he began to bellow out his resolve, " I Agarth the Mighty shall take up this task in the names of the God of…hic."

    That was all he managed to spew out before another man came behind him and knocked him unconscious with a weak blow to the back of the neck. This new guy was much different from the rest of the lot as he seemed to be a man of Britannian or Roman descent. He was the youngest of the unit seemingly just my elder by a few years. He was also seemingly much smarter than his comrades for he was the only with enough sense to wear a chainmail shirt underneath his tunic. He stepped up to Elaine and I and bowed his head in apology, "Forgive my friend Agarth for making such a display for your loss, but I give you my word I shall do my utmost best to retrieve your son."

That man had a certain genuine look in his eyes that made me trust his words for face value, a first for me when it came to any other person aside from Luciana. Even Elaine was taken back by the man as her grip around my hand loosened the moment he stepped forward. Her interest in him was of no concern to me, and besides I had known for years that women were fickle creatures subject to change as consistently as the seasons that come and go. Also I could not blame her for her apparent enamor for this man. He was a well groomed individual with short blond hair and a light goatee that made him appear even older than he was. Couple all of that with a well built frame of a fighter and I'm sure if I ever brought this guy to the brothel then all of the girls including Mother would be all over him.

Another Saxon who much more sober than his previous friend came from behind the well groomed man and gave me a dirty look as he knocked the well groomed man upside the head.

Now this one was the stereotypical Saxon that I had heard so much about. The man was built like an ox and looked like he had never eaten anything but pure beef his entire life. His thick beard and lack of hair only helped to promote the image that I had always envisioned when it came to the Saxons. Though his dialect was not nearly as rough as the first person I heard, it was still a challenge to make him out, but thankfully Elaine was able to perfectly grasp what he was saying and then recite it back to me in a hushed tone, "The man calls himself Varna and shall accompany you and the one he refers to as Cub on this hunt for our son."

Varna and Cub huh. I was simply hoping that one of

them would tag along with me, but two just made my task much easier than I had imagined was possible. Out of the two, Cub was obviously the weaker and would thus be the focus of this plan. By then, Elaine had handed me a cloth that I was able to wrap around the wound on my face to stop the bleeding for the time being and while it would have been better to fully attend to the injury on the spot, I had to sell this façade of a father so concerned for his son that his own life didn't matter. I bowed down gratefully to the two men for offering their assistance and then proceeded to tell them of the job they were taking on. Out of all the parts in my plan, Elaine and I had figured that this would be the most difficult part of the deception due to the fact that I had to ensure my story didn't conflict with the knowledge and beliefs that they had on the area. The last thing that I needed to happen was one of the villagers claiming that I was lying and then I would have to rely on my old methods in order to negotiate with them.

With the village of Dale being located so close to the land of Cambria, the notorious bandits of that region had made it a habit to venture south into these parts to stock up on whatever goods fit their fancy. In the last few months since I arrived at this town, there had been a significant increase in bandit activity. Normally they would have posed a genuine concern, but such things were just a way of life these days. An attack from a bandit horde was just as expected as a thunderstorm. Still, the recent rise in attacks had been the source of many of the fears that the villagers had tried their best to bury, but those same fears served as the perfect scapegoat for the blame concerning the kidnapping of Galahad.

It had not been the first time that the villagers had heard of those bandits participating in such depraved actions, so this was certain to gain their support.

And thus I began to recant the tale of how Galahad was taken from me by these vile criminals and how they deserved the justice of cold steel as retribution. I amazed myself at how fluently I told the tale. I half expected to have to have to gather my thoughts multiple times, in order to keep everything together, but everything just fell into place the moment I began to speak. I could feel the pride that must have been radiating off of Elaine as I skillfully integrated all of the lessons that she had taught me into my story. The villagers around us were all tearing up as I continued my tale, and at the end of it I was proud to say that I convinced them of the validity of my story. The Saxons seemed to possess no interest in the details aside from the location of where I told them the bandits were, so once I was done the two men assigned to me quickly gathered a couple days worth of supplies and began their trek to the eastern neck of the woods beyond the village.

I was able to breathe a sigh of relief as the realization of the first step of my plan had worked better than I had expected. The only part left to play was the farewell between Elaine and I before I set off to rescue Galahad. It took a little time but after a few moments we were able escape the tons of condolences given by the villagers and have some time to ourselves. We hid ourselves underneath the shade of a weeping willow towards the outskirts of the village where I was finally able to free my hand from her grip. I couldn't hide the smile from my face as I embraced her within my arms.

She nestled her head against my chest as she tightened her grip once more around me before I pried myself free of her. I eased my nerves as I began to speak to her, "Elaine it all went exactly how you said it would. Now everything else should be simple."

When her eyes finally grasped how excited I was for this chance, her face obtained a stern look quickly as she stepped away from me. She looked up towards the hanging branches of the willow as she pleaded, "I know that this is all you have wanted, but try not to forget that my son's life is at risk for you to realize this quest of yours."

"This quest? This is not some foolish adventure to find treasure. I'm trying to save an innocent life! You should be honored to help me on such a noble endeavor where you are actually using your skills for something worthwhile."

"Oh yes of course. I must have forgotten that you killing three Legionnaires looking for you as you hid here is such a noble endeavor to take pride in. Wasn't there also that messenger you boy that you threatened to kill if he didn't give you that message to Merlin about your whereabouts?"

"All of those were necessary."

"And what if my son's life becomes necessary! I swear Lancelot if he comes to any harm…"

I grabbed her by the neck because I was tired of her condescending tone as her vexing words continued to flow freely from her lips.

"If you think I would ever forsake a child as innocent as Galahad for my own desires, then I suppose that you don't know me as well as you believe yourself to. Now go back home and be quiet you ungrateful harlot!"

With those last words said between the two of us, I made my way to rendezvous with Varna and Cub. The two of them were busy chatting by the time I arrived so it took them a second to take note of my presence alongside them. Once they had figured that I was there, it was Cub that seemed to take the most interest in what I was wearing. It was only a quick glance, but in that one instant I could tell without a doubt that he was examining my worth as a fighter to see if I would be a burden to him. I must have given him no cause for concern since he didn't say another word to me after the inspection although he did take another glance back to get another look at *Fang*. Unfortunately, I could not afford to bring my other weapons along with me due to the fact it may easily raise suspicions on why a simple villager in a relatively peaceful town like Dale would find the need to carry a short sword coupled with twin daggers as well.

Along with the lessening of any armaments that I would have normally carried alongside me, I also made a note to lessen the extravagance of my attire to the level of a simple villager as well. That day all I wore was a faded brown tunic along with a pair of worn down trousers that I borrowed from a neighbor that exuded obvious signs of field labor, and while it may have been a better idea to replace *Fang* with a simpler and cruder blade, that was just something I couldn't allow myself to do with a clear conscience.

I gave the two of them a friendly greeting before I took the lead in our little party to lead them into the wilderness that surrounded Dale. As I passed the two of them, I paid close attention to how Cub's hand never once left the handle of his blade. His fingers were wrapped just tightly enough so that he would be able to quickly draw his blade at a moment's notice. This one was a cautious fellow to be sure. It seemed as though my earlier thought was off based because of the two of them it would be most certainly him that I would have to be wary of the entire time because if I gave him a good enough reason he would most likely cut me down without a second thought. I thought back to the smile that he showed off when we all first met, and realized that the soft spoken mannerisms that he displayed earlier on were likely just a façade to lower the guards of those around. And while many of these assumptions may have been presumptuous, something in my gut just told me to be wary of that one.

 Before we left I had instructed them that the bandits had been rumored to have a fort near the border of Cornwall edging into Bristol Channel. The journey by foot was estimated to take around five to six days considering how Dale, though close to the channel geographically, had no roads or legit paths to connect the two. This disadvantage would make our journey have to cross though the wilderness as we pressed toward the Bristol Channel. The first portion of our journey was for the most part quite uneventful as we remained in an eerie silence of one another, well aside from Varna who would continually go on humming some vexing tune from a Germanic folk song. Day after day passed by as we followed the trail that I had convinced them was that of the bandits and for the initial leg of our trek they had no qualms with following me blindly, but after a couple of days with no results and not even a sighting of one of one of these bandits that I had mentioned. Varna had begun to get anxious. The wilderness of the Cornwall region of Britannia was by far the most notoriously dangerous place in the land that had become the breeding ground of many tales of mythical creatures and monsters that became the common talk of many taverns during the night.

There was no doubt in my mind that Varna had heard of at least a few of these tales as he continually scanned the area for any sign of danger approaching. Cub on the other hand remained steadfast and calm throughout the entire first couple of days. I couldn't blame Varna for his growing anxiety because most days we traveled late into the night due to the fact I continued to play my role as an overly concerned father searching frantically for his son. During those days, our path consisted of not just strolling through the woods but included scaling a couple of low cliffs, crossing a river, and taking a shortcut through a cave. All of which had drastically reduced Varna's stamina by the seventh day.

Three days later I suppose he had finally reached his breaking point as he threw down his axe in frustration one day as we gathered our possessions from camp. The man had an odd look of desperation on his face as he came right up to my face and grabbed me by my tunic. Cub tried to step in, but Varna shot him a crazed look that made him step down reluctantly. His attention then turned back to me once more as he began to give me an earful, "Listen here Briton! We have been following your lead to this bandit camp you swear by your mother's life that is in this direction, but after ten days we have seen not even a hint to tell us you're right. Well I'm tired of waiting and wandering aimlessly. I'm done following your lead. We do this my way now!"

Varna threw me down on the ground and picked up his

battle axe once more and began to pump it in the air as he walked around in circles calling out, "Hey bandit scum, stop hiding behind your mother's skirts and come out here and fight us like men, so that after I kill you I can take your sisters and wives as my prize!" He continued this rant for another couple of minutes, and the only thing I saw move during that time were a flock of crows that he scared away with his thunderous voice. When he finally quieted down, his face was flushed red and slightly dripping with sweat. He looked my way and laughed for a second and then his smile quickly faded into a cry of pain as an arrow was released into his shoulder. Varna fell to one knee and Cub and I drew our blades and took cover behind nearby trees as we tried to pin point the archer. A few more arrows were fired at us as we maintained our cover, but could still not ascertain our attacker's position. I looked over at Varna and saw he had taken another arrow in his leg and struggled to limp away. I smiled as a streak of silver flew through the air towards Varna. He turned in just enough time to witness his impending death, but was saved when Cub jumped in front of him and deflected the silver arrow with his shield.

Cub continued to hold his ground as arrow after arrow flew by aimed at Varna yet each and every one of them was blocked. While the save of his comrade was a touching scene, the act was a foolish one that gave away his position for the archer to continue trying to pick the two of them off. The good news though, was that with another body in the aim of that hidden archer that allowed me to sneak up on him wherever he was. I slowly went to my stomach and began to crawl through the underbrush as I put some distance between those two in me. I tried my best to make the least amount of movement as possible to ensure I maintained the element of stealth but my cover was nearly blown when a pair of legs quickly streaked past my face. My heart stopped as the leaves from his trail were kicked in my face. I peered back to see a man covered with rags with dagger in hand making his way to outflank Cub and Varna. My initial instinct was to go and aid them, but I stopped when I thought about making the same naïve mistake that Cub had made. If I went to help them, then all I would be doing is exposing my position as well and make me another susceptible target for this archer.

They were nothing but swords for hire, so I had no intention of helping them at the cost of my own life and goal, yet I found myself off running after the flanker in just mere seconds after I had shrugged off the idea. The flanker was quick to say the least, but he was not nearly as fast as I was when it came to straight line speed. As we came back into same area of Cub's final stand, I saw that the flanker had succeeded in getting to Cub's blindside and by then Varna had passed out due to his wounds. The next sequence I executed without a single thought as I came from behind the flanker with *Fang* in hand. He had no idea I had come in his blind spot as I slipped *Fang* underneath his chin. I didn't even give him time to react as I slit his throat in one quick motion and then went back to back with Cub as I waited for another flanker to possibly show himself.

Cub showed no signs of dismay or even surprise as I leaned against his back and after deflecting a couple more arrows I heard him chuckling, "Well it seems as though you were leading us too well towards the bandits. You could have at least made a mistake so that we ended up behind them by accident instead of surrounded."

He must have noticed it a few moments before I did as I witnessed glimmers of iron swords reflecting the rays of the sun every now and then. I counted around ten men in total and then winced in pain as an arrow made it past Cub and grazed my shoulder. I leaned my head further back so he could hear me clearly as I spoke, "If we split in two directions I can take half with me while you handle the other half. That's our best chance as of right now."

"One against five for each of us huh? Those don't sound like bad odds, but if we leave then that archer will go for Varna. You go on ahead and try to save your son. I'll hold them off here and protect Varna."

I was stunned. Was this man one of those simple folk that I had seen come into the brothel every now in being treated by some of their village friends or did he truly have a death wish. No man could possibly be that noble to risk his own life in such dire situations for the life of a man that was fading by the second. I had seen many men that preached to have the same noble virtues as that guy, but when it came down to it, they always displayed how selfish and self serving people really are. That one though, I could feel the unwavering conviction behind his words. He had every intention of protecting his comrade even at the cost of his own life. While escaping from this situation would have been fairly simple for me if Cub did indeed stay, I could not live with myself if I allowed such a man to die while I escaped safely.

When we had first left Dale, I had every intention to do

this, but now under these circumstances even I hesitated to go through with my plan. My doubts ceased once I thought of how these were the same men that had Luciana and I had to save her no matter what the cost. With that conviction firmly placed in my mind, I drove my blade through Varna's chest and then responded to Cub, "Now you don't have anything to hold you back. We need to split now if we are going to get through this."

The blood from the mortal wound I had inflicted continued to flow out onto my blade as I removed it from his body. While Varna may not have been the first man's life I had taken, he was the first I had killed in cold blood. Any sentiments that still lingered were quickly buried as I found myself blocking the attack of another bandit that had tried to catch me off guard. I met the incoming slash of his sword with a downward block, and then delivered a head butt to knock him off guard. As I drove my blade through this man as well, I felt his entire weight fall upon me as the last bit of life slipped away from him.

Luckily the man I had just killed was concealing a bow on his back which I quickly liberated from his possession before I discarded the body. My eyes were able to quickly spot one of the arrows that had been deflected and I scooped it up along with a handful of dirt as I notched the arrow and then let it fly off in the same direction the other shots had come from.

A few moments passed us by until we heard a resounding thump as a body fell off one of the branches of a nearby tree. The moment we heard the thump Cub drew his longsword and we both proceeded to taking the fight to the others in the woods. As I entered the woods, I was immediately surrounded by three more bandits all with brandished iron swords bearing their fangs at me. Before they were able to attack me all at once, I closed in on one of them and delivered a precise slash across his neck all the while snatching his blade from his hand so that I was now wielding two.

If my days among the legionnaires had taught me anything, it was that no circumstance was unsurpassable. My child like skills with the blade had been drastically improved to the point where there was none among the Legionnaires that could best me and those two bandits would soon fall into the same grouping as the others. Whether they came at me high or low, individually or together, fierce or cautious, the result would always be the same as I took little time in besting them both before they even knew their lives were gone.

With those three disposed of, I knew that left six more that I would have to handle. Cub was the more heavily armed among the two of us so it made sense that more would go after him as a precaution. While the guy seemed more than able to handle himself, I was sure that six was far too much for him to handle. Just before I went off to rescue him, I heard the crunching sound of twigs breaking and quickly turned around with my swords drawn ready to strike. To my surprise stood Cub with his own blade drawn with hardly a scratch on him, in fact the only sign that he had been recently in battle was the fact that his blade was still freshly coated with the blood of those whom he had slain, but there was no way he could have managed to beat all six that were left?

After I noticed that the blade was still drawn, I realized

that the number of foes he defeated was the least of my concerns at the moment. I took a step back and he took one forward with his blade still pointed my way.

He had the same distrusting look in his eyes that he displayed the moment we had left the village. While Elaine would have tried to talk her way out of a situation such as this one, I figured that no silver tongued words would ease the rage that he no doubt had towards me. If some man that I had never met before killed a comrade of mine as I tried to save him, I would have reacted in the same manner. He had every right to want to fight me, and thus I decided to honor his request. He took a step back and in a surprisingly calm manner spoke to me, "Why? Why did you take Varna's life?"

Merlin had once tried to teach me that if an opponent was too busy asking questions rather than trying to take your head, then you owed him the honor of answering any of his pleas before you ended his life. Out of all his ridiculous teachings and sayings he taught me, that one was one of the few that hit home. Thus I answered his question truthfully, "He was dead weight and I would not allow some Saxon imbecile that didn't know the meaning of stealth and who showed no concern for my son to stop me from being able to save him. I apologize if his death has caused you grief, but I shall not apologize for the action that I took."

"Despite how cold your actions are, they are understandable so I bear you no ill will Lancelot, but the fact that you have taken the life of another being in cold blood while not defending yourself causes me as a soldier sworn to uphold the laws of King Mark to deal you the justice you have brought upon yourself."

"So you are a member of Mark's army, and you point your sword at me in the name of justice rather than simple vengeance. While I too have sworn to uphold a King's Justice as a Legionnaire initiate, I believe that in order to act upon the King's justice in the most pure way one must be willing to take that justice into one's own hands."

"It is the vigilantes like you that sow discord and unrest with your self-righteous attitude that has caused us to have to rely on the aid of outsiders for military aid."

"And it will be the discord and unrest that I sow that will in turn save the life of an innocent woman whose life is not viewed as worthy of King Uther's and King Mark's protection. So if we must fight then let us do this now and cease to waste anymore time."

"Agreed. Rest assure though after this is over I shall still return your son to his mother."

"A nice gesture Cub but it is one that will go unfulfilled. Before we begin though, I would like to know the true name of the man I am about to kill since I'm sure that your parents had more sense than to truly name you Cub."

"My name is Arturious of Cornwall, but you may call me Arthur."

"Arthur huh. That is a name that I shall surely remember

*Chapter Six*

# Romans

IT WAS A name that I would indeed remember and hold with high reverence for the rest of my days. The thought of killing him was a stale one that the harder I chewed on it the worst the taste was. But I quickly made my peace with the notion as we both drew our blades, or so I thought. Despite the dearth of fear I had, my hands still clutched so tightly around the handle of my blades to the point where the carvings on them were imprinted on my palms. The weather was in a soothing state of autumn, yet there was a chill that would not leave my bones. That kind of fight was one I was not familiar with. Up until then, all the fights I had partaken in were for survival or training, but that encounter was not a fight about hate or senseless killing but one of honor, a lost concept in those days in Britannia. It was a strange feeling to point my blade at someone that I harbored no ill will towards but he stood in the way of me saving Luciana and that's all the motivation that I needed to endure the burden.

Dusk had long since settled in leaving an auburn glow upon the land. Even Arthur's hair had a faint residual glow to it. I took up my stance and waited for him to take up his. As he did, Merlin's words echoed back to me.

*Knowing your opponent is the first step to winning the battle. Take notice of every subtle detail he makes and allow your body to react accordingly. Remember this and you may just make Legionnaire.*

There had not been a single day when I did not think back to the tutelage of the old man in some regard, but in that instance his words, while once hollow and reminiscent, reverberated loudly within my soul. It was at that moment I keyed into Arthur's stance with the perceptive detail of a hawk hovering over its prey: sword drawn, shield raised to cover his face, knees bent with legs slightly apart. All of which were a signature style that that Romans were famous for in battle. Seeing one that was not a Legionnaire engage in that style was truly a surprise, if I were a lesser man then I might have been worried.

 Both of us dragged our feet through the autumn leaves that had made their bed on the ground as we paced around one another still. He kept he shield raised like a true warrior that had seen countless battles while I held my blades steady and unwavering with my resolve to do what was needed. As both being trained to be professional soldiers, we were both well aware of the fact that the first strike sets the tone for an entire dual. Our breathing was scarce and our eyes never wavered from one another.

 When I was a boy, I would have had the patience of an infant when it came to battle. I rushed in fool heartedly with the utmost confidence in my own abilities. While I had every right back in those days to think that way because of the weak competition I faced, Merlin soon showed me the error of my ways when I left with him.

The words that Merlin used were that I fought like a hungry street urchin, a description that was not too far off from my actual position. I may have had the wins to hoist, but after watching me fight for a brief time he stated I would fall against any opponent that had any real training. Talent certainly did course through my blood he told me, but...

*A man can't be great off blood alone. Only with blood and the sweet smell of sweat can a man be great.*

Day after day, he weeded that mentality into me as he sparred against me to display his physical and tactical dominance over me. One by one, the truths that I had held self evident when it came to fighting were slowly eroded until they were naught but pebbles in my path. It took some time but eventually he did indeed impress the truth upon me that I was a long way from being able to pride myself in being a real fighter. The cruel irony though to this day remains that the moment I decided to admit that truth to him myself was the moment in which my life turned for the worst. Merlin was by far a man that lacked a certain sense of common human traditionalism. During the first week following his announcement that I would be his apprentice, Legionnaire after Legionnaire expressed his condolences which I had at first taken for the loss of my home.

Instead of conducting my Legionnaire training in a normal

fashion, he went with as he calls it a more exotic approach that was sure to offer all of the trails I would need to overcome if I wished to be Legionnaire. His brilliant idea was none other than a generous stay for in me the wilderness of Cambria on my own for several months as I struggled to survive. All he gave me at that time was a just one of my daggers and the promise that during my stay he along with other Legionnaires` in the unit would randomly attack me, and if I was ever captured then I would not be allowed to join.

As Arthur's shield thrust itself towards my body, I took a couple steps back and felt the nudging of a tree root brush against my foot. This allowed me to quickly sidestep the blow and watch with a grin as Arthur slammed his shield into a nearby tree. The impact from the slam without a doubt must have numbed his shield hand as he quickly dropped it and put some more distance between the two of us with his blade still pointed my way. I hacked away a hanging branch impeding my path so that I could maintain a clear sightline. The leaves from the tree he struck danced around us before they touched the ground in silence.

My time in that wilderness had indeed prepped me for such a challenge like this as Merlin had forewarned. It was due to that time that I now was able to constantly take in my surroundings.

This time around I took the lead and closed the distance between us and followed up with a sequence of quick slashes that he managed to block efficiently. My blades resonated against his sword and shield as the intensity of my strikes picked up. Not once aside from Merlin has an opponent defended against me so efficiently.

*Only those with a cool head and resolute heart will prevail in battle. If you lose either of these you are doomed.*

Merlin was not the kind of man whom you took advice lightly from. I cooled my nerves and backed off from Arthur which gave him enough time to regain his shield, a sacrifice I was willing to make. It was at that time when things intensified. With another simultaneous charge of our blades, I thus began in the hardest fought exchange of blows I had ever undertaken till that point in my life. Sweat began to spill forth from my body as we continued our dual and my eyes tried their best to keep a firm grasp of his movements, but he moved with such skill that it was a challenge to just stay on the defensive let alone strike.

As my body began to ache, that's when an opportunity to end this dual arrived. Arthur slipped up and briefly lost his footing as he evaded a strike I had intended for his knees. It was during this moment where my destiny from that point on was set in stone. In that instance where victory was at hand, the chill in my body returned. It was brief: perhaps a second or two at best but it was long enough for me to pull back and allow him to regain his footing.

The two of us just stared at one another for a moment with a cold silence shared by the woods. The grunts and scowls that had once been on our faces were replaced with slightly rosy cheeks and two pairs of distant eyes skirting around one another. The silence was broken by a soft laugh from Arthur that I found perplexing. All the same though, I found myself joining in with him for a succinct time before his laughter was replaced by a muffled scream. The bushes behind him shook vigorously as a large man scared by burns across his face and right arm burst through them. Stems from the bush rocketed through the air followed by miniscule berries hardly yet ripened. Arthur froze as a dear would when it spotted a hunter but struggled as fiercely as a moth entangled in a web as the man wrapped his arm around Arthur's neck. It was no wonder that Arthur could not break free from the man's grasp due to the difference in sheer size between the two of them.

His eyes briefly met mine as they cried out for help, but my only response was to sheathe my blade. The shock on his face was understandable as I called out to his captor by name, "Bors, impatient fool. Now if only you'd go after women with such enthusiasm then I'd consider you more of a man."

I motioned my hand telling him to ease his grip and he humbly complied but not before responding to my earlier tease, "Forgive me Cousin, it's just that every woman, whether poor or rich, fair or foul I encounter has already shared her bed with you. And mother always told me to never play where the dogs have been."

"Anyone you would call mother is about as visible as that God you so piously serve."

"Please raise your hand if your mother is a whore…well that's awkward it looks like you're alone on this one Cousin."

"You're such a prick, but all the same it's good to see you Bors."

"Ay, it's been far too long. It is by the grace of God that you have managed to keep yourself alive all this time."

"More like by the grace of my blades."

"One day I hope you will open your eyes to the truth Cousin, but until then I have come in regards to your letter. All the instructions scribed within have been completed including the safety of that sweet child Galahad."

Bors truly was one of the few men in this world I could wholeheartedly trust. An unprecedented amount of tension flowed freely away from my body as those words left his mouth. Compelled to rest, I proceeded over to the tree Arthur had slammed into beforehand. The walk over there was a bitter sweet one as the soles of my shoes left parts of my feet exposed to the vexing occasional pricklings of pinecones and twigs that now littered the ground. My back found a particular comfort about being able rest against the dampness excreted by the growing moss, but I had to close my eyes to avoid direct contact with the lingering rays of the sun as it continued to make its final decent for the day.

A smile emerged across my face as I marveled at how beautiful the world looked right then in that moment as the words that Bors said to me echoed through my mind. Just a little more I thought just a little more until my journey to save her would be complete. The peace of mind I had so rightly deserved fell to pieces as Bors called over to me on what to do about Arthur. By that time, Arthur had been firmly bound by Bors' impressive knot work, a skill he no doubt learned during his time serving as an aid to a Roman soldier. My eyes glazed over Arthur and focused in on Bors' as he took a firm seat on Arthur's back to stifle any hope of escape. My eyes closed once more as I addressed him, "Bors' the man is not one of those peasants that adore you in Bamburgh. I'm pretty sure he doesn't like the idea of having you crush him."

"Like I care about the needs of some dirty Britons, you of all people should know they only exist to serve our needs."

"Oh, yes the oh so troubling needs you face of not being able to wipe your face and lace your boots. Ah, the life of a noble is such a strenuous one isn't it?"

"Perhaps you would appreciate it more if you weren't gallivanting the countryside playing Legionnaire. Putting your life on the line for a dysfunctional nation with nonsensical ideals, is not my idea of a life, and worst of all there's no profit in it."

"Self sacrifice is such a silly eastern ideal after all. It's not like any people you revere have done such a thing. Anyway go ahead and get off of him we're leaving."

"And leave him alive?"

His words stabbed my sense of honor so deep that it was difficult not strike Bors with the back of my blade. Once the impulse had subsided though, I saw the logic in his words. Arthur was the least to say a nuisance I had no idea how to properly deal with. Any other man I would have simply executed and went on about my merry way, but the idea of killing him still made me stutter.

"Just leave him out here. Too many deaths may cause unwanted questions among the Free Riders hindering the plan."

"So him simply disappearing and you coming back then won't further complicate things. Look, Lancelot obviously this man must have let you drink from the Holy Grail or something like that to make you hesitate not once but twice.

Frankly, it's disgusting to see you exercise such mercy towards a mere Briton."

"Your lack of clarity ceases to amaze me Bors. If you bothered to pay attention to how he looks rather than what land he stands on, you'd see that he is obviously of Roman descent."

Bors took heed to my words and examined Arthur for more than just five seconds this time around and pathetically fell to his knees. If it disgusted him to see me show mercy, then imagine my disgust to see him beg for forgiveness over such a trivial concept such as origin. His apologies came to an abrupt end as Arthur finally decided to speak his mind on the issue concerning himself and what was going on. If it had been me, I would have asked for answers much sooner.

Arthur asked, "Who are the two of you? I know not whether to think of you as the best of friends or enemies in collaboration with one another. Either way though, all of this talk about me is distracting all of us from the real issue at hand: your son's life Lancelot."

Bors nearly began to choke on his own laughter as he put the finishing touches on Arthur's entrapment around the base of a tree. As he began to observe the work he had done, he spoke with less understanding than an infant as he continued to laugh, "So…sounds like you finally slipped up and have a brat of your own to tail you around. Maybe now the concept of toiling the land you bought will now kick into gear."

"And maybe the concept of my blade in your throat will finally reach my mind", I responded sharply. "But no, he speaks of Galahad. He believes him to be my son with all good reason on my part."

The deceit that had been looming over Arthur finally

poured down and soaked him with just the first stage of the plan I had concocted months ago to save Luciana. There was little doubt in my mind that the desire to kill me out of his misguided justice would soon dissolve into a bitterness that would seek the rage filled vengeance of his comrade. I waited for his eyes to intensify and stare at me with abhorrence, in which I deserved, but his crystalline eyes never faded to black nor did they mark me with contempt. Instead, they opened up wide and looked at me with a look of pity rather than rage. His voice was mellow when he spoke, "So was this all for that woman you spoke of earlier: the one abandoned by both kings?"

Bors on the other hand gave me a look of ignorant distain. Per usual he had assumed the worst of the situation. I paid neither of them any attention as I gazed out toward the forested horizon as the blanket of sunlight stretched over the land began to recede. Night would soon be upon us and I did not know these woods to the extent to where I favored being out in such conditions. Bors would not agree with the notion of staying put, but such an impasse between the two of us would be highly disregarded as usual.

I called over to him, "Bors, its time you showed off your marvelous hunter skills that you honed while behind the plush walls of Bamburgh and secure of some game as I set up camp for the night."

His reaction was a predictable one as he contested, "Make camp? Surely your time with the Legionnaires impressed some semblance of common sense, or did they only teach you how to paint over the Roman flag with new slightly different colors and fly under a new name."

"Be my guest Bors if you'd prefer to be the dinner of a pack of wolves. On second thought, go ahead I can use you as bait to lure them away from us. Worry not though, I'll be sure to remember your sacrifice every time I'm looking at our newly painted flag."

"Just make sure you remember me back when I had all of my hair and without these scars."

His words made me take another hard look at the state his head was in. His pure white skin had become charred as the marks covered the right side of his face extending down to his right arm. The burn marks had healed nicely over the years, but the fact still remained that they were a horrendous sight for the common eye. I couldn't see how Bors' could still manage to look at his own reflection with the same content he once had years ago, but never once had I heard him curse the mark that had been bestowed onto to him because of his kindness towards me.

Despite all of the jests and the insults thrown, I cared for no other man more than I did Bors. It was rare to find a soul so loyal even amongst family which by blood relations we were not. Bors had been an orphan boy in the Roman capital whose life had no purpose until my father's brother came along and took him in as his own. Apparently my father hailed from a prestigious Roman family that even had its own estate in Britannia.

For years, Bors attended to my Uncle's every need as his steward, and he was rewarded with the kindness of being named his son after an injury in battle had rendered Uncle impotent with no heir to call his own. Bors claims to have met my father for the first time after that adoption had been made. It was right after he was recalled from Britannia and left Mother and I to die that he found himself facing another unwanted nuisance in his life. Apparently father hated Bors with a passion that only Poseidon could conjure on the harshest stormy night.

    Bors has always been quite aloof with the subject of my father. He told me once that my father simply put was just a very angry man. Those were the only words into his character that I was ever allowed and the presumed final words on his death bed proved such things. After taking a fatal injury in battle from a Saxon, Father revealed that he had bedded a Persian girl in Britannia and she now bore him a son. While other parents may have revealed such facts out of guilt, Bors says that Father said these words proudly as he looked Bors in the eye and laughed as any idea of him inheriting Castle Bamburgh shriveled away. It was with those dying words that Uncle and Bors ventured to *The Lady of the Lake* to find me. The memory of their arrival was a vague one that Bors often has to remind me of,but I seem to recollect Mother arguing profusely with Uncle about taking me away. It was a warm memory in my heart that showed how much she could not bear to lose me, but what I do remember was my first encounter with the stocky boy of thirteen that said I looked like a rat. His words had caused us to get into our first little scuffle with him making me look the fool in front of Luciana. I know not whether it was the tear streaking down a dirty three olds face or if he saw a little of himself in him, but from there on he treated me like a brother. It was from his rough and rugged tutelage that I learned how to fight and the true value of something beautiful as a blade.

    Bors and Uncle came several times after that over the

next couple years until Uncle finally gave up and said that Castle Bamburgh would be placed under Bors' care until I came of age and wished to possess it. I know not all the deals that were spoken of between Mother and Uncle, who died shortly after leaving Bors in charge, but I Bors never once complained of his role as the steward to my castle as I grew into age. He had every reason to shun and even hate me, but he never did.

Distance, I had never desired to be alone with such intent as I did at that time, but Bors would not allow me such moments of weakness. His singed fingers mowed their way through my hair as he gave it a hard tug that nearly lifted me off of my feat. The pull of his fingers without a doubt still left the same aching sensation as if it had been my hair reduced to ashes. He soon released me and then trotted off into the woods to no doubt gather some firewood and perhaps a meal for tonight. Despite the burning pain still coursing through my scalp, he left me with a smile on my face per usual whenever he pulled my hair like that.

Much to my preferred liking, the rest of the evening with Arthur went by without another word said between the two of us as I set up camp. During its initial stages, I found the silence of the woods comforting as it reminded me of home. As time went on though, the silence did indeed become a tad maddening as the more I thought of home, the more I thought of Luciana and what cruel conditions she could be enduring. Painful thought, after thought crept into my mind with each image being more gruesome than the one previous. Finally when I could bear the tortures of my own mind no longer, I turned to Arthur.

Night had blanketed the sky by then on that starless night with naught to light the land around us aside from the roaring fire from the camp. My shadow flickered constantly as I made my way to the tree that had been Arhtur's home for the last few hours. Just as he had been earlier, Arthur still slept with his head dangling slightly as he waited till the morning for his fate. When I had noticed prior in the evening that Arthur had become susceptible to sleep, I was amazed. At no time in my life whenever the conditions surrounding me were unfavorable, did my mind allow me the ease of a peaceful sleep, but him, he just stood there eyes closed head slightly tilted as if he waited for a volley of arrows to rain down upon him.

 I doused him with a little bit of water from my canteen and surprisingly he woke slowly and with as much energy as a cat. Water droplets still dripped from the tips of his hair when he looked up at me. I moved so quickly as I drew my blade that I gave not even a single drop time to wet the soil at our feet as I drew *Fang* towards his neck. At first I thought the splashes crashing on the steel of my sword were drops of sweat, but alas they were the mere drops of water from his hair. Either he felt no ill intent from me as the steel edge of death grazed his neck, or he was a man unbeknownst to the concept of fear. I pushed my blade slightly firmer against his neck, until I saw the edge glisten with trickles of crimson red.

 I was blunt and straight forward with my question as I asked him. "What is your true aim in working with that group of Saxons? I'm quite intrigued to why a devoted soldier for King Mark who is well versed in the art of Roman combat is working with that band of thugs."

I could see that he possessed no desire to tell me anything, but in this situation a man's desires were often an afterthought.

With hints grogginess still in his voice, he explained his purpose to me reluctantly, "While I was bound to secrecy by my King, it seems as though I have not much of a choice. From what I take of your conversations with Bors, I can assume that you desire to join the ranks of the Free Riders for your own personal reasons. I on the other hand am acting out of the commands handed down from he who I call my liege Lord and King. There had been rumors circulating that a band of Saxons had been abducting woman and children of all ages from the lands of Albion and Cornwall. We had become privy to no other information aside from that and after the reports began to increase we decided to take action."

"So you're working as essentially a spy looking for the whereabouts of these missing women. On your own that is a bold move I had not thought King Mark was capable of. Perhaps I had the man pegged wrong."

I retracted my blade from his throat and took a seat by the fireside. The words of men were fickle ones and hardly deserved my faith in them, but his words not only matched up with tales I had heard myself but I failed to detect any sort of deception on his part. I watched the embers from the fire float pass my eyes as a wind came through and chilled my core to the bone. The fire lost much of its life from that sudden gust of wind and struggled to stay alive.

"So what of you then Lancelot?, said Arthur. Why is it that you have gone to such measures to join this band of Mercs? While I mean no slight against King Uther, he hardly seems the man to care for as he calls *mundane* affairs as he strives to unify his broken land."

"I see no need for me to tell you of my interests especially since I still find myself at turmoil to whether I should let you live or not."

"While I know you have no reason to trust my words, I beseech you to take heed to my words regarding this matter. No matter your goals, I have been with this group for the last few months and am more than capable in answering any of your questions regarding them."

"Trying to augment the values of your life huh? Fine, I'll give you a chance to prove your worth to me. What do you know of a woman named Luciana?"

The moment I said her name there was a slight change in Arthur's disposition. While most would not have taken note of such a minuscule difference, I did. I could see even afar in his eyes that her name meant something of great value. I had expected no such reaction when I mentioned her name, but the game had changed now. I feigned a level of disinterest as I continued to gaze at the kindling fire. His response to me was a timid one with a tone full of concern.

"Why would you be interested about her?"

I held a twig out toward the fire and turned it slowly as I watched the tip blacken until it slowly ignited. I tossed the twig aside and watched as the once fragile limbs of it dwindled away to black ash.

"She is someone very dear to me that I gave something to long ago. I heard that she is a captive of your Saxon friends."

"I cannot say that I've have seen or heard of a woman

among the lot. The name at first sounded familiar but now I cannot say."

The man was a liar. I could see clear as day that he was hiding something. A few years ago, I can say for certain that he would have lost a few fingers if I still possessed that impulsive nature that acted on my emotions. Now though, I could analyze the situation and decide on the best course. Perhaps they called him Cub due to his overall naiveté because no matter how hard he tried to hide his uneasiness he still maintained a certain innocence about him that made him easy to read. When we first met, noticing such a thing was nearly impossible, but fighting with a man has a certain way of revealing his true nature

"Well according to my source, she is in camp with your band of plundering brothers. So forgive my rudeness as I don't take the word of a soldier of Cornwall over my own gut. If your words hold true, then either she was there before you joined or she is dead and either outcome will result in the deaths of all those greedy Saxon pigs that you roam with."

"Once again I..."

Arthur suddenly stopped once he saw Bors return with some game. He had done well this time around by managing to take down a doe. I glanced back at Arthur who shied away from eye contact with either of us. He was a smart man indeed. He could see from being around us that my mind was one that would be much more willing to compromise or strike a deal if I saw the advantage in doing so. Bors on the other hand…once he was rooted in a certain belief no amount of tugging or pulling would uproot him from his belief. Any chance that Arthur had of being free lied with the whim of me granting him mercy or using him further. The shadows cast off by the trees around the fire loomed over Bors' right side making his scars look ominous as he began roasting the doe.

He flashed a brazen smile my way with his voice full of pride, "The Lord was gracious to me once more Cousin as he provided us this magnificent doe for dinner."

I pinched the pile of ash of the twig I burned early and rubbed the ashes between my fingers and the last grains of it scattered back to the ground leaving my fingers as blackened as the Berbers I had heard tales of to the south of the Roman Empire. I subsequently began burning another twig as I jested toward Bors, "With a catch like that, I'm starting to believe more and more in your God. There's no way that a lumbering fool like you could have managed that."

"I doubt you could have fared better. You'd be too preoccupied to maintaining your hair to focus on tracking this specimen."

"Well someone in this family has to look good to make a reputable name for us."

"And here I thought your mother was doing an excellent job by herself."

"The name of the Lady of the Lake has indeed spread far and wide. I remember when I was younger she used to simply be Vivian the Temptress or Nimueh the Maker of Miracles. No matter how far I have gone in my travels there is always some fool out there religiously spouting off vivid tales of his night with the "Great Lady"."

Bors must have been touched from my words because he responded sincerely.

"Worry not Cousin, once your plan goes through your name will be on the lips of every man, woman, and child in Albion and even Cornwall."

"Kindness is not your strong suit Bors. Your words would be better suited for those whom fill your pockets priest."

"Unfortunately, salvation comes at a price. Just as our Lord paid the price with his life, so must we."

"The world is full of darkness and the only light in it is the shine of a coin. So do you understand what must be done tomorrow?"

"Yes, I shall be gone at the crack of dawn whilst you still sleep. It shall take me a few days to return to the fort where I can tell my comrades how you decimated our numbers."

"Yes, during that time I'll put little distance from here and wait to be captured. Once that part is done, just make sure you secure Galahad and wait a fortnight till we make our move."

Bors flashed another eerie smile which made me want to cringe. Time and time again, I told that man to tone down on those looks, but I let it slide that time since I knew how excited he was for tomorrow. Bors if anything enjoyed bringing about his "righteous" condemnation upon those he deemed as wicked. So it was no surprise that he had memorized the plan to the finest detail: a comforting fact indeed.

The first phase had gone without a hitch and now I prayed that tomorrow would hold the same outcomes as well. I doused the last remnants of the dwindling fire leaving nothing but the light of the moon to light the wilderness. Bors and Arthur by now had given way to the dreariness I'm sure was caused by the day's events. I took my leave of the two of them and traversed through the wilderness until I reached an alcove free of trees. That alcove seemed to be as Bors would no doubt exclaim a safe haven for those worthy of the Lord due to the fact the entire area received the direct light of the full moon looming in the night sky. Its pale moonlight was further enhanced as it reflected off the drops of dew in turn making the entire alcove glisten brilliantly that night. The night air was still like the night air of the island on the lake. How I remember night after night venturing towards the shore with Luciana and simply staring up at the stars that lit the sky. To do so alone was a somber feeling. I don't know what prompted me to do so, but I pulled out the letter I had sent Bors months eariler. The parchment was wrinkled and in far worse condition after being stuffed in Bors' knapsack for the last few months.

*To my favorite fool,*

*I pray that you are well and haven't let your lush castle life fatten you up…well even more than normally. I know it has been some time since you have heard from me but things have changed since I no longer am considered a member of the Legionnaires. Those selfish fools have proven to be a sham of the of the once illustrious warriors I had once believed in. With those qualms put aside, I find that I am in the need of your help for someone very dear to me has been captured by a group of Saxon mercenaries. Despite my overwhelming urge to carve my justice for her wronging onto their bodies, I realize that this situation requires a more delicate touch. After much deliberation I have discerned that the best option to ensure her safety is to join the ranks of these men and then save her from their filthy clutches. In order to do so though, I will need to set in motion a series of events that will leave their group weakened allowing me a spot to join. For that purpose, I come to you to beseech you to join the ranks of a group of notorious bandits in Cornwall housed in a fort near the Bristol Channel. I hear that their leader is a vicious bastard whose head will prompt my name to be received with great recognition. So join their ranks and learn what you can. My next instructions will come within the next fortnight.*

*Lancelot*

## Chapter Seven
# Melwas

**THE MORROW CAME** and I found the campsite without a certain pious fool to agitate me further. If it were not for the chill that lingered in the morning air, I would have found great comfort and being eased by one less burden. With no clue to when Bors would arrive at the fort, I knew it would be best for me to leave camp as soon as I was able. Unfortunately, the original rations of the journey had been depleted this far along, and it didn't help the matter with that fool taking half of the little I had left as well.

I would be in need of food and water that could last for the next few days. It was the days like that when I found myself missing Elaine and Mother the most. How I wished I could just call upon them to feed me, but this time around I'd have to fend for myself. Even though I called myself gathering my things, my possessions were a bare minimum with the only real items of value being my blades, but it seemed as though I had almost forgotten one vexing piece of baggage I had no clue what to do with.

Hardly enjoying his quality time with the tree, Arthur

had a gloom look to his face even while he slept. The thought crossed of taking him along with me, but he had proved to be far too worthy of an adversary. If he should decide to turn against me, then I'd be in trouble once more. While hunting was not a sport I preferred to take up often, I knew that if need be I could catch some game fairly quickly. I left him with all the confidence in the world that I'd return quickly.

It wasn't until a full day hence when I realized that my hunting skills might have a tad overplayed in my mind. To say that it was a rainy day when I returned to the camp would be an understatement. It was still quite early in the morning and the wispy, cloud covered sky cast a grayish tint over the entire land. I could scarcely see the land before me as I felt around my surroundings to get a grasp of my position. My wrinkled fingers easily dug into the wet bark of the trees before me. I had lost count of how many splinters I had. The constant drops of rain splattering on the leaves around me was all I could concentrate on as I remembered many a night sitting by the window of the brothel with Luciana listening to the droplets.

My memories were washed away with the last bit of dirt on my body as the rain finally came to an end right around the time I returned to camp. Soaked head to toe with water logged clothes and the shame of barely managing to catch a thing, I limped over to Arthur, who as I had expected was still a captive of the tree. Arthur's face had grown to an unpleasant pale texture that showed obvious first signs of pneumonia. If he continued his exhilarating vacation on that tree, I'm sure that would be the end of him. His hands and arms had the bloody marks of one trying to free himself to no avail. His hands were stained with a tint of crimson that not even the rain could wash away, he must have been trying to escape for quite some time.

His mind was barely conscious when I approached him. Eyes fogged and with little signs of life sparkling in them drew further attention to his condition. I saw no need to sully my blade with his blood even more now since he would die on his own in no time, but his words continued to resound in me. Now matter how much he tried to feign his knowledge, he knew some information on Luciana.

The world would most certainly embrace the idea of equality among men before I allowed the chance, no matter how minuscule, to save her pass me up. I sliced through the fine knot work that Bors had always been so proud of and caught the cold, stiff figure that had once been full of life.

As I had discerned earlier, Arthur was well built and would be a cumbersome burden to carry any other way aside from slinging him over my shoulder like a casket of wine. It was too bad that his inner contents wouldn't yield the same bountiful reward as a casket, but for the time being I had no qualms with carrying him in such a way. The direction in which we would set out did not matter as long as I made sure that I made as little progress as possible while leaving visible tracks that could lead those bandits right to us. That was the one good thing about the rain. I was sure that without even trying I would leave very impressionable tracks in the mud of the forest.

As for the element of time, I had little issues to worry about. My body may have been well trained and strong for my slender size, but to haul another grown man around that was even larger than I was a feat that no doubt delayed any sort of progress I might have had. And thus we traversed through the wilderness with no destination in sight for a good few hours into the morning before the dead weight placed upon my shoulder finally decided to grace me with his presence. His awakening moans were that liken to a boy whom had just hurt his ankle as he struggled not to cry. It gave me a certain sense of pleasure to see that this was how King Mark of Cornwall's warriors awoke each and every morning. I'm sure that Merlin and the others would tear up as their laughter consumed them if I ever told them of this tale. Well I supposed they would have been if I were still liable to join their ranks. Those who left the Legionnaires for whatever reason were viewed as the human embodiment of cowardice and treated as a plague to all those who still bore the chest plate and straps of the Legionnaires. And it was even worse in my situation with being known as Lancelot the Black, killer of all legionnaires.

Before Arthur had completely awoken, I found refuge within a small cavern. The bones of small critters remained scattered across the remnants of a long forgotten campsite. Once my baggage had begun to squirm a little more, I laid him against the wall of the cavern. My body ached as I took a seat of my own on the floor and spread out my body on the worm and beetle infested soil. Arthur's drowsy moans finally evolved into coherent words as he fully opened his eyes.

"Lancelot", he said with an air of pleasantry. Whether he was happy to see I hadn't killed him or if he was happy to just see that I had come back for him I couldn't tell. I much preferred the former than the latter, but if so I have always dealt swiftly with men that in which I had found fancy in their eyes towards me. It's amazing how diplomatic a piece of cold steel could be.

The next thing he did was take in his surroundings almost simultaneously while stretching to work out any kinks left over from his vacation. He still exuded obvious signs of weakness that would need to be attended to. For a moment, I felt my stomach tighten as I thought back to the decision I made to leave him behind when I went hunting.

His eyes gazed up at the sun's position in the sky before he spoke to me once more, "How come we have stopped this early within the day? Should we not keep moving to cover as much daylight as possible?"

Had this man no idea of how far I had to lumber under his weight as I carried him through these woods? The first words out of his mouth should have been ones of praise and gratitude for not only sparing his life, but for also enduring such lengths for him. Typical, no matter what corner of the world that people hail from the primary thought on their minds will be of their own well being.

I responded back quite harshly as I tried my best to invoke a sense of guilt, "Sure that would be ideal if I had left you to die on that tree, but out of some unforeseen sense of compassion I decided to spare the tree that kind of burden. Besides we are not trying to run away from anyone. We want them to catch us"

Arthur's head sunk deep into his knees as he muffled his amusement.

"I had hoped that you and Bors had partaken in some wine last night when you spoke of getting captured."

"Wine you say? I suppose you're right. But my wine is far different than the one you're accustomed to. The wine I have partaken in the past few months is an exquisite brand called vengeance and retribution. It actually in all truth serves more as a hard liquor whose taste is rough but once you down it the drink it leaves your body with a satisfying sensation. So in a way you could say that our thoughts have been diluted by this liquor, but I'll keep on downing it until I see no more of a need to."

"Vengeance you say, a powerful force yet an empty one at that. It is liken to pleasure being found with a woman between the sheets. At the time nothing seems as powerful and desirous, but when the moment is over you are left with emptiness and somewhat of a shameful guilt as well."

"I have no idea what women you have been with, but as for me all the ones that have allowed me to warm their beds have never left me with such emptiness the following morning. On the contrary, it is always those mornings in which I always feel most alive."

"Such a mindset will only lead you down a path of ruin."

"You're starting to sound more like Bors now Arthur. Fair warning, the only thing that has kept my sword from his throat was the fact that he is family. You do not hold the same privilege as he does for spouting such philosophical nonsense. The world we live in is not ruled by sweet sayings or conniving words but rather cold hard steel. You'd be quick to learn that Arthur. Remember I spared your life on a whim and others won't share that same mercy."

"I am well aware of the mercy you showed to me and

I intend to repay you in full. So then what's our next step then?"

His words did not fall upon deaf ears but it was the response that earned nothing but silence from me. The words that I wanted to speak just didn't only not come but they weren't even formed either. My mind was as blank as those countless apology letters I had tried to write for Luciana and Mother. There was an awkward silence between the two of us as we looked at one another until I just laughed and walked toward the opening of the cave. Making such decisions has always been a pain for me.

"We wait. It's been enough time for us to be on the move. It's only a matter of time before they catch up to us."

"And then we raise a white flag and beg for mercy."

"Too bad they won't know that they will be unwittingly signing their leader's death warrant."

"Or we could very well be signing or own."

You may be signing your own. But I have no plans on dying until I save Luciana. I wondered if cowardice was a quality shared by all of King Mark's warriors. I may not have agreed with the beliefs of the Legionnaires, but if anything, I admired their fearless conviction. Whether it was due to the fight we had or the fact that I had been a part of his brief bonding time with that tree, there was an awkward silence between the two of us. He must not have been used to just waiting patiently for something to happen for his legs were fidgeting incessantly while he leaned against the rocks. Such movement had always been a vexing sight for me to behold.

Luciana had a bad habit of that leg-twitching thing when she was bored. It took some time but I literally kicked that habit out of her. We were also children back then, so I wondered how a grown man would react to being kicked suddenly. Unfortunately, hers wasn't as bad as I had let on to be: it was more of a visible thing that bothered me, but with Arthur…it was that sound…that mind numbing tapping against the cave floor that soon echoed through the cavern. The echoes were small enough that he didn't pay too much attention to them, but as for me I was about ready to amputate his legs. If I knew that this would be my reward for saving him, I would have left him on that tree to rot.

Just when I thought I couldn't handle another second of that noise, I reached for my *Fang* but stopped short when I pondered on the consequences. Despite how thoroughly Elaine and I had planned for this, I would be going into this next phase somewhat blind and would have to react to the progressing situation. It would be for my best interest to not erect an even stronger wall between the two of us. For all I knew, I may have a dire need for his assistance if things fall apart. In fact, I knew it would be beneficial to work on tearing this wall down somewhat before we began.

No matter the reason, unsheathing *Fang* always seemed to be an action that brought my heart comfort. In order to further sell my lack of interest in him, I stared longingly in the steel framework of *Fang*. My fingers caressed her edges slowly and gently. She was like one of the women I had grown up with. Upon first glance her cold, smooth edges invited my fingers to dig deeper into her to see if she would bite, but as they dug deep around her sides I was then able to see past the sparkling glamour and feel the wear in her. The knicks from her previous owners were becoming more apparent as well as her fading sharpness. It would not be too much longer until I found her to be useless to me. A blade should only be meant for the hands of one man: one blade to treasure as your own and maintain its sharpness. A blade that simply passes from one hand to another will eventually become dull as luster fades to rust.

There was little I found to be common between the two of us so I simply asked him, "Arthur, where did you learn to fight like that? I had thought that King Mark rejected all of the Roman ways and practices."

He gazed out into the forest while seemingly reflecting on some sort of thought, "I am I man with no true home and as such I am bound to no set rules placed forward by my King. My blade is promised for King Mark out of a sense of repayment. My teacher was…a strange man born of the land yet one who embraced the ways of others.

"Sounds like my teacher except he was more of a lunatic than a strange man." The only difference is that Merlin hated everything to do with Cornwall. So I doubted if there was anything too similar between the two.

"Yes, well though I call him strange, the man was a genius when it came to the realm of fighting, I could not begin to tell you all of the styles he is a master of."

"And of all those styles, he taught you how to fight like a Roman. How fitting for one bearing the blood of a conqueror."

"Blood of a conqueror? Well that's certainly an interesting connotation coming from one who holds the same blood."

Even in that state, he still proved to be a perceptive bastard. "I'm surprised that you were able to figure it out. So are you like me, a mut, or are you a pure blood that was abandoned?"

"For all I know I could very well be the descendant of Jesus. My mother was said to have died bringing me in the world and as for my father…that I don't know."

I'm sure that if we continued to go on with the pedigree that we each possessed then I would have told him something I would have regretted. When his eyes shifted from the golden scenery of the wilderness to my sleeping body, I'm sure he got the message somehow.

It must have been nightfall when Arthur woke me up while placing his hand over my mouth to stifle the sounds I made. His hand was moist from the cave floor and the taste of dirt lingered on my lips as he removed his hand and pointed out towards the flames dancing in the wilderness. The fiery light was no bigger than my head as it moved quickly through the woods leaving a light trail of smoke in the air. The holders of the light were naught but shadowy figures shouting a strange tongue back and forth with one another. Most likely they were Cambrian by my guess aka the scum of the island only being slightly better than the Scots.

They were a notorious people for abandoning the life of peasantry to become bandits and highwaymen, so it was no surprise to see that they were the group that Bors had infiltrated. I heard Arthur's sash rustle against the side of the cave as he tried to leave, but I quickly grabbed his arm to stop him. If we were to leave out of there in the den of night, there was a chance that we would be killed. The best option would be to remain in the cave and trust in the tracks I left to lead them here. Or those were the thoughts I wished were the first to come to mind. Sadly to say, the first thing that popped into my mind was that Arthur would not be able to handle himself in that state. Without a word uttered amongst the two of us, Arthur glanced down and saw one of the deeply imbedded footprints I had made in the ground before entering the cave. I released him as he came back in and closed his eyes as he rested on the cave wall.

Such trust. Such foolish trust he had just placed in my plan without any reservations. It was that kind of blind trust in a man that usually resulted in death. Not even I was that sure of my plan. It was entirely dependent upon how furious they were about the deaths of their comrades. I tried my best to follow Arthur's lead but doing so as calmly as he did was beyond me. I was sure that Arthur could hear the beat of my heart from where he sat. I would be a fool to admit that fear did not come to me easily. I am just like any other man. It was not the fear of dying though that made my heart race, but rather the fear of dying without being able to fight back at all.

The Cambrian shouts became more emphatic as the dancing fires came closer. Their rustling through the trees around them was done violently as the sounds of branches being cut down and shrubs being forcibly removed filled the air. They were getting closer alright and they were angry as well. For a moment, my hand went to the hilt of my blade but my new found growing common sense as Elaine called it made me stay my hand. Finger by finger I removed my clutch from the handle and dug my nails into the soil. I needed to relax or else my chances for survival were going to be made slimmer than they already were. My mind instinctively drifted towards thoughts of Luciana as if it were caught up in some sort of unforeseen current.

Soon the foreign shouts calling for my blood ceased and I was left with nothing but the image of Luciana wrapped in a pure white dress of silk. Her feat dipped into the edge of the lake with a setting sun setting at just the right angle behind her casting a glow that made her seem like a figure out of myth. Her back was turned to me the whole time, so all I could see was her long hair swaying in the light wind. My heartbeat was placated as the image of her moved on from her standing peacefully by the lakeside to her being chased into the deeper parts of the water by a youth with raven hair splashing water upon her. Soon the two were drenched with water and shared nothing but laughs as the sun set behind them. Darkness was the next thing I saw as I was woken up by the men looking for us. Just as a Mother would reach for her child in times of crisis, I went for my blade but instead grabbed nothing but dirt instead. The grimy hands of one of the filthy Cambrians grabbed the back of my hair and in response I scattered the handful of dirt into his eyes. His clutch was released giving me enough time to scurry away for a moment like a cockroach. Getting a bearing was difficult. Ever since I awoke the cavern was flooded with light that blinded my actions. The warmth of the flames only made my movements more erratic as I crawled around senselessly. The men that surrounded me had no figure yet loomed over me like shadows I could never escape from. I looked for Arthur in the confusion but found no sign of him being there. Not even a cry for help was made: only the laughter of those men along with my heavy panting could be heard.

Before I could even react further, there was a dagger to my

throat and Bors standing in the background behind a group of ragged men pointing me out in the Cambrian language.

His eyes were ones full of sorrow though he wore a painted smile on his face. I embraced for the worst. Hands grabbed hold of nearly every aspect of my body as these men who seemed to be clothed with naught but dirt and rags bound me while dragging me out of the cave. I struggled and cursed to give the look of a man of common origin that had no idea why he was being attacked by these men. I caught a glimpse of a chuckle from Bors as he watched my performance under the veil of a dark hood.

Further past Bors, was another group that had Arthur with his hands and legs bound tightly. As opposed to me, Arthur provided no resistance but tried to talk his way out of the clutches that he had found himself within. There had been enough distance placed between us that I had no idea what he was saying, but I could tell he was finding a way to aggravate them due to the fact they began to repeatedly beat him for opening his mouth. These men were just as the stories had described them: monsters that enjoyed causing the suffering of others. I could hear their wicked laughter as they continued to beat Arthur. Even Bors joined in on the festivities, a clear sign to how important they viewed these acts. Arthur was not alone in his pain for long. My hair was yanked once more from behind as I was swung around and met the fist of an unknown man over and over until the initial pains faded into a drowsy sensation as I blacked out. The last words I heard before I completely passed out were:

*"Melwas will be pleased to have their heads"*

## Chapter Eight
# Pain

**THE IRON CUFFS** chaffed my skin even worse than the stone, cold floor. The links rattled with every subtle movement that I made served as a constant reminder that I was in fact nothing but a lowly prisoner. I never once in my life thought I would be glad to be labeled a prisoner, but there I was. Naked and chained in a black cell with just as much moss growing as the stone in place. The foundation of the cell had withered down enough so I could feel the breeze of the sea squeezing in between the cracks and kissing my skin. A cruel torture for any man. I had never been imprisoned before…but only after a small amount of time in that place, I forgot what the taste of freedom was, and that breeze just made my mouth water.

As for the smell, well it was already bad enough so there was no need to add further detail in thinking about it once more. Sleep was hard enough in these conditions, but it was further agitated by the rats that would scurry on by while taking a nibble to see if I still lived. I wished that rats had an ounce of the sense of men because if so I would have killed one and left its body as a warning to the others. But they would most likely just resort to their primal nature and just devour their brother before heading my way. Despite all of this though, I was happy that I was chained there alone. If that was what I would have to endure to save her, then I welcomed on even more challenging conditions to test my resolve.

Being there in the darkness surrounding by naught but more darkness. It was a fitting place for me. I could only imagine darkness the that Luciana must have had to endure to survive if she did still live at that. Those thoughts were deep within a realm I wished to avoid traversing in, but under such conditions a mind couldn't do much else but wander. Chances were against her living. She was a beautiful girl who no doubt was the eye of all those scum's desires, but if her love for me had become half of what Mother said it was, then she would have been killed refusing men such as that.

Love, I had never once thought that emotion would linger in my mind while not attached to Mother. The tales that those men who frequented the brothel told of love did the real word no justice. In their words, love was naught but a weak word that women and children spout when they need someone to protect them. Men have no such need of a thing called love unless it was associated with the sea, rum or the warm treasure that women could offer. While I had not believed in the word too much myself, there were leagues of difference between my thought process and the ones of those men. I had thought the word to be nothing but a fairy tale expressed by those that didn't have the same blood. I could never imagine ever loving one that had no blood relations with me.

And yet it was that foolishness that was the precedent of all the events to come. All it took was one moment of weakness, a drop of the ironclad guard that I built over the years. I was young and thus there was no way I could have know of the power of being entwined within a woman's arms and legs. I was nothing but butter lying on top of a hot pan quickly being melted away. The night had been one of magic if such a thing indeed existed in the world. No words were said between the two of us only our heavy breaths grazing one another's shoulders along with the tingling sensations still crawling up our skin let us know we had done something amazing with one another. My fingers fit perfectly between hers like a puzzle that had gone unfinished for far too long.

She playfully bit my ear as I nuzzled my head against her bosom. It was a completely different feeling from when my head rested on Mother's. Her bosom was like a comforting protection that enveloped me, but Luciana's…resting my head on her was akin to satisfying a deep hunger that I had withheld for far too long. I took a deep breath as I continued to lie on top of her and soaked in her smell.

I had no idea why I became so intoxicated by her smell. It was no different than the aroma that lingered around the brothel: a strange mix of fresh fragrant roses along with the stench of stale ale. The two together made a potent combination that let all those who entered know they had found *The Lady of the Lake*. The smell was all over her as if she had become apart of the brothel now. The thought of her becoming another part of that dreaded place infuriated me as I wrapped my arms around her. Her plush lips kissed my neck and then, it was then that accursed tear streamed down my face and landed on hers. She pulled me closer and I whispered the words I that had thought to be naught but a dream.

*I love you*

I killed her with those words. I knew of the resolution that she had made, but I killed her all the same. I felt her clutch me tightly after the words left my lips. Such a sweet death I had given her, and yet I barely even remembered saying those words in the morning, or better yet I didn't want to remember. I was nothing but a selfish child clinging on to his favorite plaything when I said those words. There's no way that a man like me could ever love anything truly. I was no different than those men that frequented the brothel so often. I looked upon all of the women that raised me with a hungering eye and reveled in getting in fights to prove my worth. There was so much more too that made me ill fit to hold the love of someone like Luciana, but in the end I received it and that may have cost her life. She waited for me and kept herself pure for me and me alone while I left her and found refuge within the arms of countless more women. And I did so with hardly a second thought to her or her feelings. What kind of man did that make me? One that surely deserved being chained and naked in a cell that's the kind.

Footsteps echoed down the corridor beyond my cell and there was a rattling at my door. My first thoughts were to use the brief window when the door would open to charge whoever was misfortunate enough to be my guard and kill him, but I remained still.

*One fortnight.*

I had told Bors to allow a fortnight to pass before we made a move, and I intended to stay true to the course no matter what. The first light I had seen in a day crept through into the cell when the door was slowly opened in a cautious manner. I could not say whether the guard was one of the men that had taken part in my capture. The barbarians of Cambria all looked the same to my eyes. A slender man with his sword attached loosely to his side awkwardly came into the cell. I shot him a look of disinterest as I went to lay on my side. I took in a deep breath as I prepared myself for the worst. The man kicked my side and managed to knock the wind out of me. I instinctively grabbed for my side, but this time his foot crashed down upon my hand. I had to curl up in a ball to best protect myself from his onslaught. All during which he continued to shout in his strange tongue, but I did pick up on the name Alun shouted repeatedly. Most likely he was a friend of the mongrel whose foot was becoming far too intimate with my body. This continued till I became too numb to move and blood had begun to drip from my lips. As he left, I struggled for breath while my mind kept saying:

*It's only a fortnight,*
*It's only a fortnight*
*It's only a fortnight*

This routine between him and I continued for as well as I could tell several days. During that time, I learned the names: Alun, Aeron, Elisud, Grwn, and Huw. All these names were repeatedly spit at me during these beatings. At first my guard seemed rather reluctant to beat me. His eyes never made contact with mine, and his blows were full of grief rather than anger or cruelty. That soon changed as time went on. He slowly began to enjoy his revenge and pursued more entertaining paths to my suffering such as giving me minor wounds from his blade and pouring ale over it. The burning sensation caused my screams to echo through the corridor and my hatred too zeroed in on this man. When there finally came a day when the beatings stopped, I thought the fortnight had passed and Bors would soon come for me. No one came though. I sat in silence for God knows how long. It's hard to say which was worst during my stay there. The beatings I took from the guard I decided to name Enfys, it seemed appropriate for him, or the waiting for something to happen. The cell was engrossed with such darkness that I could barely see the outline of my own hand before me. Every second that passed seemed like an hour and every hour seemed like a day. Under such conditions it was no wonder why prisoners often looked so deranged. I wondered if Arthur was faring any better than I. After all, he was in bad shape last time I saw him. Without any sort of treatment, the man could very well have been dead.

 The silence was broken when Enfys came in once more with Bors behind him. My motions were mixed to say the least. I wished for nothing more than for that pious fool to hold him down and allow me to repay for his kindness, but I didn't know if I was to wait for a signal or not, so I held my ground. Enfys had an unpleasant look to his face that day. It was as if someone had killed his dog and then kidnapped his wife while at it. Bors...well had the same stupid look on his face as always, so I wasn't too worried about what was about to happen, but still I was concerned.

Enfys threw a tattered robe towards me and instructed me to follow him. The brown robe was barely fit to be called so with the state it was in. It seemed like one good tug would tear it in two cleanly. While I did prefer to have a sense of style, I couldn't argue with just walking out naked and bruised, so I complied and dawned the musty old robe that smelled like the fisherman that Mother would entertain. Enfys scoffed at me and then took his leave of my cell. As I walked past Bors, he dealt me a sudden blow with his fist directly to my jaw. His little sucker punch drove me to my knees and extracted a laugh from Enfys as he chastised Bors in a poor common tongue, "Bors, not that I'm complaining but why did you do that?"

Blood dripped from my lip as I clenched my fist, and that lumbering fool just stared at me before he replied, "I thought that he looked far too pretty for the scumbag that killed Aeron and the others. When he meets with Melwas, I want his true face to show."

It certainly was smug of him to take this opportunity to take a shot of me, but despite my suppressed anger, I was glad to see that Bors had managed to infiltrate the group to this extent. Anyone who would have met him in the streets would assume that he was nothing but the pious man that he preached to be. Whoever would have thought that priest by day gallivanted as a notorious bandit by night. The idea was a bit frightening on how he was able to flawlessly lie every waking second around these people. It was like putting on a mask that he could never remove. I had never thought of the burden that I had placed on him when I asked him to do this for me. A fool he may be, but I was certainly glad to be able to count on such a loyal fool as my ally.

"Well Bors despite how much I agree with you, we should let him be for now and allow Melwas to decide. If God is willing then he will receive far worse treatment than his friend has."

My fool of a cousin kicked me forward with the underside of his boot while yelling at me to get up. Loyal he may be, but I promised myself I would get him back someday for this. Grunts and moans were all I could muster as I tried to rise to my feet. The bruises left by Enfys had taken their toll on me over my stay in the cell. With the dim torchlights barely illuminating the corridor, I was able to finally get a glimpse at the state of my legs and arms. Discolored and bruised in far too many spots to keep track of, I turned away from the sight of them as I feared what the rest of me may look like.

I progressed slowly behind Enfys with a bad limp as Bors pushed me along every now and then. While my injuries were somewhat of a pain to deal with, the extent of my injuries were grossly exaggerated to portray a vision of weakness and fragility to Enfys and whoever else may prove to be a later threat. This group's hatred for me slowly became more and more apparent as we traversed down the corridor towards the stairs. After being to walk for moment, I was able to discern that they had been keeping me held up in a wine cellar of all places. For the most part the cellar had a decent upkeep with the there being little signs of decay as opposed to my cell. In fact, it now seemed as though, only my cell was the only part of the cellar had had been kept in bad condition. Never before had I felt such love exuded towards me.

I was grateful that they had allowed me to walk myself to wherever they were taking me. As we proceeded up a flight of stairs that I presumed would provide the exit from the cellar, I was able to work the stiffness from my legs. Sore and bruised they still may have been, but if need be I was confident that I would be able use they without any hindrances to my abilities. That was a lesson that I had learned well from Merlin. Adrenaline when faced with battle had a magical way of suppressing any ills that your body suffered at the time. I lost track of how many times I had to train with my body feeling like it was barely holding itself together at all.

Finally, the smell of must and decaying rats passed as we finished our assent up the flight of stairs. In its place, an aroma I had not smelled in weeks filled my nostrils with delight and my mouth with watery desires. Immediately from the stairwell, we entered a room of grand size but little decorum. The renovated *Lady of the Lake* looked more luxurious than that place did which is sad considering how lowly that place technically was. The only thing of admirable distinction was the dinner table placed in the center of the room. While the table itself was nothing special aside from the length, it was the contents placed on it that made it stand out. An array of delicacies stretched from one end of the table to the next that seemed far too classy for a mere pack of bandits.

If the food wasn't enough of a surprise, then seeing Arthur fully recovered without a single scratch on him at the table happily partaking in the delicacies lined before him did the trick. I lost my sense of the situation and instinctively looked towards Bors with a glare that obviously expressed my confusion and dismay. Clever to a fault, he hit me once again for looking his way and this time I heard a brief chuckle slip from his lips. I knew that he was secretly enjoying this. This time though, Bors did not receive any praise for his action. Instead, a resounding yell of disapproval emanated from the table. Seated proudly at the head of the table with Arthur to his left, a child with raven like hair similar to mine seated to his right, and Galahad sitting next to the child as well was a man of stout build and muscular features that made Bors look small in comparison. His blond hair hung loosely draped over his shoulders. His attire was that which respected Roman customs of a lone white tunic and leather sandals. With his immense size, I would not be surprised if when he breathed that he sudden would break free of his clothing. That without a doubt was the man I sought. That was the bandit king, Melwas.

He called forth in a fit of rage, "Bors who told you to strike my guest in my presence?"

For the first time in my life, I saw fear creep into Bors' eyes. And this was not the supposed "fear" that he held for his God, but rather true fear. He backed away from me and quickly went to one knee and his head bowed in reverence. Seeing Bors submit so easily was certainly a sight. I didn't even think he would go to his knees that quickly even if there were a flock of bare women before him, yet he bent the knee to this man without a second of hesitation. With head pressed firmly against his knee, he apologized for his action with a tremble in his voice, "Forgive me my lord, I acted foolishly without thinking. I beg for your gracious mercy."

If I didn't know better I would have thought he was praying to his God, but no there was Bors, the self proclaimed deliverer of the Word to people like myself, calling a another by the name of lord and master.

"Worry not Bors, I simply had to remind you of your place. Speaking of which, I see that my guest has sustained some rather unpleasant injuries against my wishes. If I wanted him to be beaten or interrogated, I would have done it myself. So speak who among you had the gall to beat a defenseless man bound and chained."

I saw Enfys pull at the collar of his shirt as he nervously took a step back. His eyes shifted towards Bors with a glare that seemed to hold tints of anger, sadness, and perhaps confusion. Bors just looked on without paying him much mind. Enfys remained silent by either choice or he may have been too petrified with fear. The king like figure at the head of the table spoke once more, "Fine. Since you two have less courage than my son, I'll have to ask my esteemed guest. You there, the one called Lancelot correct?"

The fact that this behemoth knew my name was a discomforting one. I began to wonder if the plan was in peril, but I couldn't afford to jump to conclusions so I pressed on accordingly. I tried my best to sound as weak and beaten as I could as I responded to him, "Yes, sir I am known by that name."

"Good, well then Lancelot tell me which of these men if not both are the cause of your injuries."

Now the look that Enfys gave Bors made sense. He was

afraid that this may happen where I had the power to persecute him. Despite how every bruise and scar called out for me to crucify him, I withheld my anger and decided to string this along for a little while longer.

"Sir…well…I don't…remember too well."

"Enough with that nonsense! Tell me or so help me God."

I quickly realized the source of Bors' fear. This was not a man to be trifled with. My hand quickly pointed out Enfys as I tried my best to display a look of victimization. His eyes glared toward Enfys as he stood up and unsheathed his blade. Enfys stepped back with his entire body shaking in fear and anticipation. Melwas then turned his eyes quickly my way as he tossed me the blade. My first reaction was to catch it, but instead I clumsily fumbled for the blade and allowed it to fall to the floor. Melwas sat down once more and spoke, "Lancelot in these parts my word is law and those who disobey are subject to trial. You claim that my subordinate was the one to inflict you harm against my wishes, so I hereby grant you the authority to exact your justice or die trying."

If a man has ever found himself at a cross roads before, then I found myself at a complete branching pathway. Never within any of the outcomes of my plan had I foresaw such a circumstance. Any normal man and even myself would want nothing more than to take Melwas up on his offer and enact my own brand of justice. But if I were to traverse down that path, then I would allow the very man I had come to kill to know of my skills. I had only a few viable options before me at that point and every one of them had to be made within the next few seconds. I didn't even have to look at Bors to know if I turned on Melwas right at that moment then he would be by my side. But the matter of Arthur remained a mystery as well. The fact that he showed no sign of injury or torture indicated that he may well be in league with this man now. I was good, but not good enough to handle both Arthur and Melwas.

If I continued to this act of mine and refused to fight, then he would perhaps be even more cautious of me than if I actually fought. What kind of man would pass on the chance for vengeance against his jailor…very few and those that did were immortalized in Bors' Bible. If I reacted in such a meek manner, then I would just add an layer of mystery around me. There is nothing more dangerous than the unknown by your side, and I'm sure a man such as he would know that all too well. The final option was to fight and kill Enfys like every muscle in my body wanted me to. The fact remained that Melwas knew my name and that for some odd reason he was interested in me. So it may very well have been possible that he knew who I was. I was stuck and unable to make a decision quick enough. It was good fortune that Enfys made the choice for me.

While my mind was off lost in contemplation, he took the chance to strike at me. In his mind, it only made sense that I would choose to kill him for what he had done to me. It was the soundest decision on his part, but too bad for him it was also the most foolish as well. My body reacted without any thoughts of the future as I blocked his attack.

After all of that time he spent beating me, he must have obtained the absurd idea that I was a weakling that had no chance in a real fight. He thus put all of his force into one strike he had expected would finish me. This truth was made prevalent after I blocked his attack when his entire body was thrown off balance. Even Galahad would have had more caution when attacking. It was in this opening where I saw the solution to my predicament. It passed through my mind quickly, so I had no choice but to act upon it at that moment. With the blade Melwas had tossed me firmly in hand, I delivered a powerful thrust into Enfys' gut. The strike was true and just as I saw the life fade from his eyes when his body fell limply against my own. And just like that all the pain that had been dealt to me by him had been repaid, but hardly in full.

Time had been lost to me by then, so I could not recount how many hours I had spent curled up on the ground in pain. All of that suffering and I was able to only make him pay for a moment. If this was the justice that Melwas spoke of, then it hardly seemed right or fair, but I was happy to have that happen. Now I knew when dealing with Luciana's takers I'd have to take my time making them pay, so that I could feel that I had obtained my due justice.

As I pushed Enfys off of me, Melwas' applause rang through the room a little too loud for my liking. It was as if he was glad that I had killed another one of his men. When his clapping came to an end, he outstretched his hand, "Now tell me Lancelot, did you feel satisfied to see his death delivered by your own hands?"

While the feeling of vengeance was empty or rather unfulfilled, I had to admit that I was satisfied to have killed that man with my own hand. The thought scared me for a moment, but I had realized long ago when I ran away that I was just as evil as the other men that frequented the brothel.

I responded simply," Yes, yes it did."

"Now wouldn't you have been enraged if some highborn fool that had never been treated as a prisoner all of his life gave the sentence to him instead and allowing you no form of retribution?"

"It's only human nature to right the ones that wrong you."

"Indeed it is Lancelot. Too bad your friend Arthur doesn't agree with us. Come take a seat at my table I invited you here to converse with us not to sully your hands with more blood."

I had thought my branching pathways had narrowed down with Enfys' death, but this man just continued to expose more and more paths. My better judgment advised against it, but I had this lingered want.

*This nudging desire of....Curiosity.*

It was something that I had deprived myself of feeling for good reason. It was a desire that often led to one's own downfall, and I wanted no part in it whatsoever, but this time I decided to act upon it. There was much that intrigued me with this man, he who slowly crept towards death's door with every moment he allowed me to live, he who commanded fear and obedience in Bors' heart. I wished to know just who this man was because he was greater than some simple bandit. I took my seat across from Arthur and next to Galahad with my chair tilted towards Melwas just in case he tried anything. I felt Galahad's hand reach for mine under the table, but I ignored the wanting touch he so desired. If anything, I had no idea who Melwas thought I was. All he had was a name, but a name hardly told the story of any man. Until otherwise, I decided to ignore Galahad and focus on Melwas who was the real problem at hand.

Despite my uneasiness towards that man, I couldn't help but fixate my eyes on Arthur who still sat calmly by eating his meal in the face of all that had occurred. Never once had his attention shifted from his plate during the fight with Enfys. He just sat there simply enjoying his meal as if there were no other actions ongoing around him. Friend or foe, nothing had changed with Arthur. He still scared me more than anyone else that I had ever known.

## Chapter Nine
# Camelot

**MY FOCUS WAS** more intent on Arthur than I had intended for it to be. In any other case, I would have noticed when a boy threw an apple at my head, but in this case I was taken completely by surprise when it struck my head. The hit hardly caused me any real pain, but I still nearly drew Melwas' blade on the child. It was the gargling laughter of Melwas that stayed my hand for I could not help but laugh as well when presented with such a ridiculous sound. The laughter came to an end when Bors came to the head of the table and bent the knee once more for Melwas as he asked to be excused. Melwas granted his request with the simple wave of his hand, but before he left us for good Melwas asked, "Bors did I not post you to be Lancelot's guard primarily and with only *slight* aid from our departed comrade?"

Bors stood between me and Melwas with his back to him at that time. He had a hard time hiding his smile as he replied, "Sorry my lord, he claimed you had told him to relieve me and to be honest guard duty is a real bore, so I didn't question his words."

"Is that so? I suppose we can't verify the dead now can we? Very well you may go."

Bors, that cunning little saint, I could easily see now why Enfys had looked at Bors with such distain in his eyes. It was Bors who was supposed to guard me, but he had managed to either trick Enfys into doing it knowing full well that he would beat me the way he did. No...there was no way of knowing that Melwas would react in such a way...unless he had seen this happen before in the past. I took another look at him as he walked by and saw he still could not wipe that stupid smirk form his face. The look of Enfys' face played back through my mind. It was a look of pure betrayal. The priest had done well and played his cards right because whatever he had done or said managed to get me at that table only feet away from Melwas.

But there still remained the issue of how he knew who I was. Either my initial premonition was correct and Arthur had indeed sold me out or there remained another unaccounted for detail. I was traversing on a pathway laden with glass that I had to be sure not to step on. No matter how he learned of my name, the key was still Arthur. Melwas had taken an interest in him regardless of the circumstances, and so it would be in my best interest to find out why. Before Bors left, he had made a point to take back the blade that Melwas had given me leaving me unarmed and defenseless as well. With no steel to guard my life, all I could rely on was my words to act as my sword and shield in this situation. Though Elaine had taught me the art of the tongue specifically for times such as that, I had never envisioned getting myself in such an incommodious situation.

One wrongly uttered word could bring about certain death to me. So I decided to start things out simply as a way to gauge Arthur's loyalty to me and remind him of his debt to me along with our original goal.

I tried to sound as enthusiastic as possible without going overboard, "Well Arthur it seems you are doing much better. I had thought the worse may occur as I carried you to the cave."

Arthur finally managed to quit stuffing his face long enough to look at something other than his plate. He used his napkin to wipe away all of the juices that had accumulated around his mouth: an obvious sign indicating his high birth or association with nobles of such class. His smile was plain and indiscernible as he replied, "Yes, it seems like I had caused everyone here quite a deal of trouble with my condition. So I thank you all for your hospitality and inconvenience."

Nothing yet everything I needed to know was taken from his words. I could still not pinpoint whose side he stood on at this time, but if there was one thing I knew about Arthur from our time together it was that he had the diction of a common soldier. He may have a refined air about him, but his mouth while decorous held the same words as mine. What he had just said at the table was a man who was speaking strictly under restraining circumstances or in other words one who was being polite out of fear of disrespect. At the end of his thank you he flashed the same smile that he showed off when he claimed to know nothing of Luciana.

*He was hiding something*

"Well as long as you have made a fine recovery then that's

all that matters." I turned my attention to Melwas, "I thank you sir for helping my friend and treating us as your guests here."

Melwas nearly erupted with laughter at my statement. In fact he was nearly in tears as he addressed me once more,"Albion and Cornwall must have some peculiar customs if being beaten senseless and imprisoned makes you a guest."

Melwas reached for a piece of meat and tore into it like a lion ripping through its fallen prey. "Let's get one thing straight here kids. You don't get to sit at the head of this table without going through as many enemies and trials as I have. You think I have never been spoken to in such a way as this? Guests and thank yous at that? Let's not be coy like girls gossiping around the stable house and act like the men we are. I'm full aware that you hate me for the treatment you've had to endure, and if not then the tales your son tells about you are grossly exaggerated Lancelot. *Guests*, don't be ridiculous. You both are responsible for the deaths of valued members of my troop and thus nothing more than my prisoners. If you must thank anything, then thank my curiosity that has allowed you both to keep breathing."

Son...Galahad! Now it all made sense. Galahad, that's where he found out about me, but still Galahad had strict instructions to not speak to anyone aside from Bors when he was captured. How could he betray such explicit instructions? I looked his way looking for answers and he turned away in shame for my searching gaze.

What am I yammering on about? Of course he didn't follow the instructions I had set in place for him. He was only a boy. There's no way I should have ever relied so heavily on his portion of the plan, but it was something that I did without a second thought. Something must have happened when Bors was with Arthur and I to Galahad because Bors said he was safe…he said he was safe! Restraints, common sense, caution I threw all those concepts away the moment that I realized that Galahad may have been placed in danger. My hand slammed down on the table as a vivid display of my rage, "Melwas, I swear if you have done any harm to this boy then I'll…"

Melwas cut me off with another outburst of laughter while pounding the table himself, "See now that is how men have discourse at the table. A man is to eat and drink and demand what he wants and exclaim what he feels. We have no need for pretty words to hide behind for only cowards hide."

Arthur apparently couldn't help but chuckle as I stared at Melwas in shock and while I didn't know it back then but somewhat in awe of his words.

Arthur stretched his hand out towards me as a plea for me to relax, "Now, Lancelot no harm has come to the boy. In fact he and Malegeant, the son of Melwas, seem to be getting along marvelously. So there should be little worry in your mind about Galahad's well being. It seems that even that man who was here earlier…God what was his name…. Bors, yes that's it. It even seems as though Bors has taken a liking to the fellow."

How cute Arthur, how cute. It seemed as though for the moment you were one that I could consider my ally. Still, I had no plans to allow my guard to drop around him for this too may have been a clever plot by him. I rubbed the spot on my head where the apple had struck and then looked towards the brat that had thrown it, Malegeant. The brat had not made eye contact with me since the incident and kept his eyes focused on solely his plate in similar fashion as Galahad had done. From his visage, he appeared to perhaps be Galahad's senior by a few years and his superior by a good bit of muscle. The son of a notorious bandit king, I'm sure that his upbringing may have been almost as interesting as mine was. In fact, due to how similar our raven hair was I could have passed him off as my son far better than I could for Galahad.

My hand reached out for his shoulder, but I caught a glimpse of Melwas' eyes following my movements very carefully. My hand slowly retracted and found its rightful spot on the edge of the table as I spoke sincerely to Malegeant, "So it seems that you have been good to my son. I thank you for that."

The boy remained silent and hardly moved an inch from his position as he continued eating. I didn't know if he was trying to be smug or just acted out of fear, but either way Melwas soon interjected to answer my question, "Don't waste your time on the lad Lancelot. He has no intentions of speaking with you because I told him not to. My boy has a bad habit of not knowing when to control his sharp tongue and I'm sure that if I allowed him to freely speak his mind…then we'd soon have one grand ole bloodbath on your hands because you would kill him, I'd kill you, Arthur would kill me and my men would kill Arthur. As you can see it wouldn't be pretty."

Another subtle mention that Arthur was still my ally in this endeavor, but all this one did was make me even more suspicious. How could Melwas just allow two people he considered his enemy to dine with him and his own son at that? Was Galahad's presence here supposed to serve as a bargaining chip for me to remain docile? I felt like the game here was constantly shifting and changing into something that had no concrete shape or form, something that I would never be able to predict. While the thought of it had my heart racing out of fear, I was still excited nonetheless. This man, this man, I wanted to see exactly what he had planned. So once again against the better judgment that Elaine had instilled in me, I continued to play this game the way I preferred best. I reached for one of the dinner knives: its edge was sharp and with enough force could easily be used as a potent weapon. I began to twirl it around with my fingers as I laughed at Melwas, "Kill me huh, I thought that you had learned exactly who I was from Galahad. Then you should know not to talk with such a confidant tone."

"Oh yes, the boy made sure to mention to my son how his father, the hardened and vicious legionnaire, could easily defeat me. At first the boy's exuberant tales of your skill were cute, but over time it became an annoyance to the point where I had to see for myself who this Lancelot was. And once you had killed off the squad I sent to find you, I had become quite intrigued indeed. Here I had envisioned a man of great stature that portrayed the very definition of power and to my disappointment you are nothing but a boy who even looks far too young to have fathered a child his age."

"I hear that the dragon that King Uther killed thought the same thing about him before his head was impaled with Uther's sword."

Melwas once again found himself erupting with laughter but as he calmed down he pointed his finger at me while addressing his son, "See Malegeant, this how a man is supposed to be: fearless and proud. These are the kind of men that will populate our nation."

I may not have known the man for very long but I knew exactly of the ideal and he spoke of. This "nation" he spoke of was no doubt the same one that the lowlifes at the brothel spoke of. Ever since Uther killed the dragon and united some of the warring chieftains to form Albion, there had been clamor among those of the various thieves dens and pirates to do the same: create a nation for them and only for them. A nation of cutthroats and robbers: it was a ludicrous idea but there were some foolish enough to dream of it. Melwas appeared to be one of those fools now.

"So you're one of them huh, one of those deluded fools that believe in this notion of creating a Camelot."

"So you have heard of it I see and I see that you too are one of the fools that believe that such a utopia is beyond the reach on man."

"Utopia, how could a den of scoundrels and murders call any nation they form a utopia?

"Hmph, scoundrels you call us and as thieves you mock us and shun us, but tell me were men born to be thieves and pirates? And if so where were all of these men during the time of Roman control? These men who you look down upon are nothing but the regular citizens, the farmers, the butchers, the bakers that once had a place in Roman society, but what were they to do when the Romans left them to fend for themselves? If there was one thing that the Romans made sure to imprint within our minds as Britons, it was that those who were strong enough take and those who were weak enough give it up."

How dare he! Is he somehow trying to justify the actions of those that murdered and pillaged villages and raped the women young and old as an act of necessary survival? How twisted could one's mind become? But still…

"You speak of nonsensical dreams Melwas. If you and those you apparently represent wished to be returned to a life of protection and purpose, then you should have moved to Albion."

"And be a lap dog of dog of that Roman Uther. No, we were painfully taught the mistake to trust in a Roman to lead and protect us. In fact, I hear that Uther hardly even protects those who he considers to be a citizen of his territory."

He had a point there. It was becoming more and more clear that the growing nation of Albion was an attempt to recreate Rome and only those of true Roman birth were allowed a chance to prosper under the protection of Uther and his Legionnaires. My entire crusade even now was due in large part to Uther's lack of concern of his own home front. When Rome left, there were those among their ranks that saw the freedom and opportunity in staying. Those that had once been naught but a common foot soldier forced to serve the Centurions to pay off a debt were now free to become apart of a higher echelon over the Britons. King Uther was the one to lead the movement to stay in Britannia and after his accomplishments he naturally took control and spread his rule slowly across the land of previous Roman territory. The great chieftains such as Merlin, Leodegrance, Lot, Ector, among others that bent the knee to his rule were rewarded the title of Lord and their men the title of Legionnaire for Uther. It was with them that Uther constructed Albion. Despite my own issues with Uther, I would gladly serve under him rather than the anarchical rule that this Camelot would impose.

"Uther is not the only ruler you could have chosen to follow. If you hate him so much why not go to Cornwall under King Mark. He is a true blooded Briton is he not?"

"As I have already told Arthur when he and I had this discussion, Briton blood Mark and I may share, but he wishes to conform to the ways of the south. He wishes for grand kingdoms and fancy balls and he acquired his seat not through battle and blood but rather through lies and treachery. Mark may claim to have barred off his country from the Romans physically, but he opened his doors wide enough for the all the ideals that came from that land. It is time that we stand up for ourselves and our own traditions for once rather than the traditions and lifestyles of those that conquered us."

Living with nothing but the ideals that you gave yourself…those were the same ideals that I had decided to live by after I left the legionnaires. It was good for one man perhaps even an entire village but a nation? I had my doubts. Nonetheless…

"So what would be the tradition and lifestyle that you and your fellow believers would impose upon this Camelot?"

For the first time in the whole conversation, I did not see a smile or any sort of look of contentment from him. Instead a solemn look was plastered on his face.

"Power. Camelot would not be a land where words gilded with gold but watered down with treachery would decide policy and who rules. In order to create the strong, one must breed them just as the Spartans once had. It would be a land with no one policing the lives of the citizens. If a man wished to have something whether it be a certain sword, horse, or woman then all he would have to do is have the power to take it and it would be rightly his. A nation with loose laws will allow only the strong to survive, and from the seeds of the strong Camelot's true form would be born."

A land where men could act upon their base wants and desires…no wonder he garnered such respect from his men. Though we crave society, we hate the rules pressed upon us. To allow such a land to exist is pure madness. I felt I was talking to a boy with deluded dreams of grandeur. Honestly I felt as though Galahad and I could have had a much more civil and logical conversation on this matter. Still, I was able to see that no matter how foolish and misplaced his ideals were, they were sincere, and for that I respected him.

"Despite how much you make this *Camelot* sound magical and just. A country's identity is solely based off of the people that reside within it. A land of nothing but cutthroats will result in nothing but simple wholesale slaughter eventually. People are born with hearts of darkness and cruel intentions, so any land where these habits of theirs would be exalted is nothing but a fools dream."

"Yes, nothing that you said could be debated but with that knowledge would it not be the right thing to try and change things to bring out the light that people can shine. While all of this coming from a man as notorious as me may seem like an irony, one can never preach to avoid the darkness effectively without ever traversing through it himself."

"The world is a dark place and the only light in it is the shine of a gold coin. You would do well to remember that."

I could see that the enthusiasm that he once had had now all but faded and wilted as a flower does when winter encroaches upon it.

"I had hoped that you two would see the reason in Camelot and join the cause. There are changing winds blowing all throughout Britannia these days. The other bandit kings of Cambria along with myself have talked about this notion more than once, and about finding men like you two to join our cause, but it seems as though I must treat you both just as I had originally planned."

Oh so Arthur thought his ideal was nonsense as well. It didn't surprise me considering how emphatically he preached on the value of justice. It's no wonder that he would condemn such a world as well, yet…I heard him voice not one objection as I had to Melwas Perhaps they had indeed already had the same conversation, but still I would have thought that he would say at least something else. I had no more time to think on the matter as I was quickly presented with the reason why I had come here in the first place. As Melwas got up from the table, I could hear the slithering sound of steel being unsheathed from his side. Like Arthur, his sword was considerably longer than the ones I had grown accustomed to, and to be frank I was disappointed that Melwas would have a sword comprised of such common steel; in fact it may have been iron. I had hoped that I would be able to get a decent souvenir, but as it turned out the only prize I could claim was his head after all. Despite the circumstance of having the most notorious bandit in that region with his sword drawn near me, I still was able to find some humor in the whole ordeal.

"So I take it you're mad because I don't like your plan. I can only imagine what you'd try to do if I refused to marry your daughter or something."

"Whether you believe in Camelot or not Lancelot, I still intend to show you the virtues of its ways. It's simple, if you want the lives of you and your *son* to remain free, then you must take your freedom from my grasp. Lawless scoundrels we may be, but we have our code of honor. You have spilled the blood of my men, and as the code dictates to those under my rule and command blood must be repaid with blood. The rules are simple and even in your favor. We fight to the death here in this room between the three of us, but there can only be one match at a time. Meaning…"

"Even if I die then Arthur has a crack at you to earn his freedom. Quite confident aren't we Melwas."

"It is simply the nature of Camelot and the code I impose on my men. Only the strong survive."

Arthur quickly rose from his seat once he had heard the terms that we each faced. Though his eyes faced straight ahead towards Melwas, his mind seemed to be in another place entirely. He stepped forward and said, "Lancelot, let me fight him first then. That would be the best chance to come out victorious because even if I fall I will have injured him enough so that you can take him with ease. That way you are almost certain to be reunited with Galahad."

Noble Arthur, noble, but I was not some sort of wench that wished for you to come and save me. I had my own sort of pride that I needed to stand for. I got Galahad in this mess and I promised Elaine that I would be the one to get him out."

I responded, "That's quite the gesture Arthur but I assure you that I can handle him. Besides my mother always told me to try and be a hero whenever I could."

"Fine hero, just try to remember that if you think you're going to die then at least injure his legs or something."

"No need to worry, I got this."

I wish that I was half as confident as I sounded. Everyone in that room save Malegeant and perhaps Galahad could see that my body had been worn down by Enfys' beatings. The sole reason I was able to best him with such ease was due to his overconfidence and the gap between our actual skill levels. I would not have the same luxury with that man.

Suddenly he sheathed his sword once more and spoke to Arthur and me, "Well now that the two of you have made your choice, you may prepare for our duel. You have twenty minutes to find something suitable to wear and grab any weapon you wish. The armory should contain all of your needs, and Arthur already knows where it is. Now be gone and return ready to fight for your freedom."

Arthur was quick to pull me by my arm and lead me away from the dining hall and into the armory with Galahad following close behind. Why that man decided to have his armory adjacent to his dining hall was beyond me. Perhaps it had to do with his Camelot notion. Inside was a fine pair of leather trousers and boots that were a fine upgrade from my moth-ridden rags. During the first few moments, I had been so occupied with the fresh set of clothes that I barely noticed the exotic arsenal that Melwas owned. If there was a heaven, then I had found it within that armory. Weapons of all sorts lined the walls ready to aid me in my quest to bring an untimely death to Melwas. My initial idea was to arm myself with my usual combo of a short sword coupled with twin daggers, but the glimmer of another weapon there called out to my mind as I quickly dressed myself. Glimmering underneath one of the numerous burning torches that lit the room was a pair of metal hands that were seemingly on display. At first the sight sickened me for I thought it was a display of the dismembered parts of one of his victims, but apparently my disgust was obvious and Arthur found nothing but humor from my facial expression. The hands were not what I had originally thought them to be within Arthur's explanation. Instead they were a sort of metal glove that had been hollowed out and cast to fit on the user's hand. Quite literally they were a pair of iron fists.

The idea to use them over all the assortment of blades collected there was a stroke of inspiration to be frank, but it was one I was grateful for. Well to chalk the entire idea up to nothing but a whim would be off by a little. Merlin had once taught me this when it came to dealing with large opponents such as Melwas.

*It is simple Lancelot, the quicker you the harder they fall. Always remember that when dealing with these giants that call themselves men.*

And was there not anything quicker than a man's own fist? Before we returned to Melwas, I stopped Arthur and asked, "I want you to go find Bors and tell him it's time to leave. After I kill Melwas, I doubt his men will let us walk out of here untouched, so feel free to take out any men you see on the way as well."

Arthur agreed without uttering a word as he picked up a finely crafted steel long sword and shield. Galahad too had found a dagger to his liking that he pocketed. I grabbed him and pulled him close to me as I embraced his small body full of boundless potential. If nothing else, I wanted him to know that I harbored no ill feelings for his failure. I took another look at that dagger and hoped he would not have to use such a thing that day. Death is a heavy burden for a child to carry on his shoulders.

As we left the armory, I took a long look at the gloves and reflected upon the man I would use them upon. In one sudden instant their new name came to me: *Sorrow*.

*Chapter Ten*

# Sorrow

**MY HANDS FELT** stifled and trapped within those gloves or perhaps that was the sensation that coursed through my entire body as I went to face my opponent. Never before had I felt just an overwhelming anxiety overcome my body, yet within all of that anxiety I was excited as well. It had been quite some time since I had the time to face an opponent who I was not assured of victory in my mind. My fight with Arthur was unexpected, but I was still confidant in my victory even though he proved to be an admirable challenge in himself, but Melwas…every Legionnaire had heard of this man in some way or another. Ever since the Romans left, the Cambrian people have been a vexing nuisance to the Legionnaires from the very day they were formed. Their land was one full of the kind of anarchy women tell their children of to make them fear venturing into the woods alone. Countless tales of the barbarian like men with no sense of moral guidance flooded the floors of every tavern and brothel in the land. They were said to be warriors born from the ashes of Achilles himself. They were said to be men devoid of fear that possessed the power of an ox. Hearing the ominous tones that those old men spoke in as the candles flickered in the brothel made nearly everyone hold their breath.

    The tales became even worse and generated further fear when a patrol of Legionnaires was said to have been ambushed by a group of Cambrian raiders leaving only one survivor drenched in the blood of his comrades. They say that all he could mutter was the word *Demon* for a week before he put himself out of his misery. These were the men I had grown up being taught to fear, and now I stood face to face with one of the leaders of these men ready to either die by his hands or walk away with his head in a bag.

    During the time allotted to me to equip myself, he had cleared the dining hall of everything save for the curtains draped across the walls. He too had changed into a similar outfit as me with nothing but a pair of trousers on. Only difference was that while my body though cut and defined paled in comparison to his large chiseled form. A sea of countless scars were sewn onto his body that made it hard to tell where one ended and another began. Such a portrait was nothing less than an artful tribute to life that he had lived among his own ilk. Merlin and the others had once told me that the bandit kings of Cambria were perhaps the most honorable and barbaric fiends that have ever walked the face of the Earth. They hold the same faces as we do and they may even speak with our own tongue at times, but it is their minds that make them the monsters they are. While we look upon a man's outer appearance and judge his status and worth, they look at a man's body and judge how easy he would be to kill. Merlin then left me one final word of the matter.

*If you ever suffer the ill fate to face one of these men, do all in your power to run.*

With those words still clear and floating through my mind, I looked upon the man before and asked him a simple question, "How many kings like you are in Wales, Melwas?"

My question seemed to perplex him, which was no surprise. I'm sure I was the first opponent to ever ask him such a question before a duel. There was no humor in his voice this time when he asked, "Why would you ask such a thing now of all times?"

To be honest I had no clear idea why I asked such a question. Perhaps all of the stories I had heard as a child had finally begun to resonate with me as I realized whom I was facing.

"Before I came here, I knew that you were a infamous leader of the bandits in this region, but it was not until we met that I began to wonder if you were one of the fabled bandit kings of Cambria as well."

Now his humor had returned to him as he bellowed, "I see that you children of the East have heard tales of us."

"We have. Your names have been akin with fear and distraught for many children throughout the years."

"As it should be, you children of the East have become too comfortable under Roman rule and have thus become weak. While a man like yourself has certainly become an exception to that rule Lancelot, you still have no idea what true power a man can posses. Only men under the rule of the Cambrian know the true value of life, and the true value of power. We have no need for of those claiming to have the divine right of men to tell us how to live. The only divine right that we need is the sweat emitted by our hands and the blood poured from our blisters."

That I could not deny. That sea of scars imbued on his chest was indeed his divine right, his right to rule. He didn't need the authority of some invisible figure or the blood of a nameless man from long ago. As long as he had that body, his right to rule was never questioned. Even I, one that wanted nothing more than to take his head off of his shoulders, respected the battle scars that he exhibited proudly. In comparison, the scars of my battles were little and exuded only a minimal level of combat over the years.

For a moment I sighed as I looked upon Melwas once more. I had never thought my plans would come to this. In order to save Luciana, I would have to do the impossible and kill one of the bandit kings of Wales. Making matters worse in the situation was the fact that my body still had yet to recover from the previous encounters. My injured and ache ridden body against his…a challenge such as this was worth all of the trouble I went through to get there.

Galahad had faded away into the background along with the rest of Melwas' men as their eyes zeroed in on each of us even while pouring ale down their throats. Their cheers quickly fell deaf to my ears as I keyed in on the one individual that mattered.

I believe that even Melwas had finally had enough discussing with one another as he took up a fighting position. Like a true bandit or anyone else that has never had any real training with a blade, he held his sword loosely by his side with the tip grazing the ground. I took a long look at the length of his blade in order to measure the distance that I needed to maintain from him.

If my battle with Arthur had taught me anything, it was that these newly designed longswords if I may call them were much more dangerous than I had originally thought. Loosely I began to hop back and forth on the balls of the feet and raised up my hands to a fighting position as well. Melwas wasted no time in beginning his attack as he charged straight forward. My eyes zeroed in on the tip of his blade as I waited for just the right moment to evade the attack. When that time came, I quickly side stepped backward right as he slashed the blade my way. To my disappointment, I had not managed to avoid the attack completely as the tip of his blade kissed my chest leaving a line of blood cut across my body. The wound was minor and hardly caused any real pain, but it was the fact that I had misjudged the range, which really hurt me.

Melwas though had not been affected by his slight victory as most would have. As Merlin once told me, the first strike in a fight to the death always set the tone for the rest of the battle. Such words meant nothing to me when I was younger because I always made the first move and cared very little of how my opponent reacted. That among many other of my bad fighting habits were quickly replaced once Merlin got a hold of me. The first strike was the perfect way to gauge your opponent's quickness, skill with a blade, and his overall aptitude as fighter. After Melwas' strike, I had learned nothing new that I had not already known, but I had expected him to get a little cocky after landing his blade on me with one attempt. To my surprise he stayed relatively calm and composed as he watched me. Once again, he went into a charge and I watched the movements of his blade, he tried to test me as he went for the same attack once more and I punished him fiercely for it. I backed stepped the slash, but the moment that the blade had cleanly passed by this time around I leapt forward and delivered a powerful blow right to his face.

Upon impact, I felt the jaw breaking in his mouth and I wasted no time to fully seize on this opportunity. I grabbed his head with both my hands and pulled it downward only to meet my ascending knee. The blow cocked his head back, and from what I thought left his chest wide open, but as I went in for the kill shot, he slashed about wildly and created a wall between the two of us as he backed off. The tone of the crowd quickly changed as they saw that I would prove to be more than just mere amusement for their boss. Galahad's cheers were the only ones I heard as the rest of the men there fell silent.

I'm sure Melwas was regretting trying the move on me again by now as he tried to cope with his shattered jaw. I figured that *Sorrow* would amplify all of my basic attacks, but I never expected them to be potent enough to break bones with one strike. Nevertheless though, I liked it. These were made for countering an opponent's attack and apparently having devastating results if the blow was placed correctly. Melwas spit a bloody tooth from his mouth along with a little bit of blood as he let off a loud cry before he came at me..That last attack had shown me the blueprint to beat him. If I were to ever go on the offensive, one misplaced blow by me could cost me my life when going up against a blade that I could not block. In that case I had no choice but to rely on the lesson that Merlin had imbued in my mind when it came to countering.

One of his principle teachings that he had was that a swordsman was not made by the quality of his body or blade, but rather the acuteness of his mind and the perception in his eyes. Fights were won once one's opponent made a mistake that allowed his opponent to seize up on the opportunity. So his lesson was simple: just be patient and continue to evade as you waited for opening after opening. While the ideal was a simple one, implementing it was the real chore. Men, especially young men are prone to act on the impulses we receive in battle, and patience is not of those impulses.

Once Melwas reached me again, our dance began. He learned his lesson from before and came at me from a different angle while executing a series of slashes that allowed me little chance to counter him. Despite the shape my body was in though, I was still much quicker than he was and was able to evade all of his attacks without sustaining anything more than a couple of mild scratches. That was until I was reminded that I was facing one of the bandit kings of Cambria.

After I had avoided another one of his attacks, he spat some of his blood at my face and hampered my vision for a brief moment. That moment though was all he needed to remind me of the sheer power he had at his disposal. I tried to avoid the attack, but I was too slow after his dirty trick. I felt the cold iron of his blade carve through me as he made a cut across my chest once more. I roared in pain as blood seeped out from the gash he left on me. To be frank, I was shocked that I was even still alive, but I had no intention to discount my good fortune. With that much blood though quickly spilling from my body, I knew that I would not be able to prolong this fight. Even then, I felt myself getting dizzy as I reaffirmed my stance. I tried to think back on anything that Merlin may have said that would serve as a guide for the rest for the situation I was in, but nothing came to me. I was alone and bleeding out with not a single way out of this mess other than to continue to fight and pray that I got lucky. The irony of it all: all of my superior training when compared to his was all foiled by a single wad of blood that he projected into my eyes. That was a shining example why the legionnaires could never hold a candle to these men. All we had were tactics while all they had was a stronger will to live than we did.

Defeat crept its way into my mind as I thought how Mother would react when Bors told her that I had died trying to save Luciana no less. Would she be able to continue living with the thought her precious baby Lancelot had gone off to see his Father and left her all alone? No, she was stronger than that I knew that she would find something or someone to fill her void where I once was.

Then there was Bors…never mind I'm sure he would rejoice in officially being the Lord of Bamburgh upon my death. He would no doubt turn it into a chapel or something, the fool.

Elaine, now there was someone who may have missed me…well until she finds out that Galahad would most likely have died alongside me or taken prisoner by Melwas since he was *recruiting* fresh talent for his dream.

So no one would miss me in the end. They may morn, but my death would pass by just like any other and I would soon be nothing but a forgotten memory..........

*"To the hell with it all!!!!"*, I thought as I took a step forward: Mother, Bors, Elaine I cared not whether they missed, but Luciana...I had made a vow to protect her and I had no plans to die until I saved her. All of Merlin's teachings and all my plans on how to handle this man meant nothing to me at that point. I had one thought: to either live through this to become a hero or die trying as a fool. Either way it began with me charging forward towards Melwas blindly fueled by nothing less that straight foolishness.

This next part was not even something that Merlin had once said to me, but rather a man that I served in the brothel a long time ago. Now I can hardly remember his face or his voice, but I can still recount the words he spoke of a man's sixth sense. He told me of how when staring at death's door and with the reaper reaching out for you that some men unlock a sixth sense that makes them sensitive to everything going on around them. If there was ever a time to believe such a notion, then it was during the next few moments of my fight with Melwas. He reacted just as I would have if I faced a man who seemed to have lost his mind with a head on charge. He held his blade steady with one hand and once I was range he attempted a thrust straight for my face.

In a split second, I dodged the attack while I continued my charge and instinctively grabbed Melwas' wrist. The next series of events occurred so quickly I doubt that to this day Melwas still has no idea what happened. With my free hand I delivered a shattering blow to his elbow and bent it in a way I'm sure was against the normal human bone structure. In pain, he dropped his blade, which I seamless caught as I released my grip on him, and executed a quick turn while impaling him with his own blade. My normal senses came back to me in a hurry as the pain from my wound set in once more. I dropped to my knees and watched as Melwas, one of the bandit Kings of Cambria drop before the son of whore.

Everyone aside from Galahad seemingly died along with Melwas as their voices became as quiet as a sleeping babe.

It felt nearly impossible to breathe as my staggered breath caused the pain in my chest to intensify. I reached for my heart, but quickly withdrew my hand once it had been soaked with my blood. I couldn't help but laugh as I slowly fell to my back. I had been through enough battles within my brief time on this earth to know that the injury I suffered though not at that time would prove to be a fatal one. All was quiet aside from the heavy pants that I painfully exhaled from my body. I felt my eyes developing a little attitude like a child as they began to shut themselves without my consent, but no matter how hard I tried to keep them open I keep seeing darkness slowly creeping in. The peace that had taken me by surprise was quickly shattered as the cold steel of a dagger kissed my chin. My eyes reluctantly pried themselves back open to the sight of Malegeant hovering over my body with a crude dagger pressed firmly against my neck. As the boy stood over me, I heard Galahad scream for him to move, but I raised my hand and told him to allow me to handle this.

Malegeant had tear filled eyes and his clothes resembled that of a butcher that had just finished slaughtering the day's meat. No doubt that was the blood of his father that stained his clothes, clothes that were once meant for dirt and mud had now been sullied by blood and tears. His trembled like a sickly child as he tried to hold the dagger to my throat. As for me, I hardly had the strength to even push this child off of me, but even if I did I had no desire to do so. As the son of a fallen bandit king, Malegeant would no doubt be the target many others in order to eliminate any lingering remnants of Melwas' power. Within the context of a few moments he went from being a privileged child with everything laid out before him to an orphan with no possession of his own aside from revenge.

Now this was fitting: after defeating one of the most feared individuals in Britannia, I was now at the mercy of a child. I wondered if the lad had it in him to kill a man in cold blood. He was obviously scared: anyone could have seen that, but was he scared of me doing something or was his afraid of committing the deed? Everyone's first kill was a difficult experience whether it be an animal or a person. Despite how callous our nature may be at times, humans were not built to coldheartedly take life. After I had grown weary of having this blood-soaked child crying over me, I looked him in the eye as I gave a harsh reality.

"Listen boy, every second you waste trembling like a girl not only do you bring shame to your father's name, but you lessen your chances of survival. Whether you have fond memories of these men or not, with your father dead, I doubt that very many of them will stay loyal to you. Now the only reason why I haven't shown you the same courtesy that I did you father not too long ago is simply because of a passing whim, but if you do not remove yourself from my body then I assure you that you will not be alone for very long!"

I'm sure my words got the picture across as Malegeant slowly got off of me. Men that had once been loyal to every word uttered by Melwas clamored in confusion on how to proceed. There was no doubt that they thought my victory an impossible occurrence, yet there I was bearing the impossible as my trophy. I heard naught the words uttered from their conniving mouths, but I knew what they were all thinking. Who would be the one to step in control that day? Malegeant continued to walk away as the words I said to him began settle in, but before he left I imparted one last set of words for him to carry.

"If you ever wish to avenge your father's death, then make sure that you never forget my face or the name Lancelot of the Lake. Let my name fester in the depths of your heart and drive you to survive, so that one day after you have attained some level of strength you can take your revenge, but until then be gone for my sight urchin!"

The broken boy scurried off with nothing but rage clouding his eyes no doubt. Whether I had doomed the lad to an empty life or not would be a question for the future, but at that time I felt that my words had been a kindness to the child. It was fortunate that Malegeant left when he did for I felt the dizzy once more and I slipped into another deep sleep in which I feared I would not awake from anytime soon.

The sleep that overtook me was a blissful one that held no remnants of pain, but rather was filled the sweet tune that Luciana used to hum when we were children. The tune, she said was one she heard a sailor sing, but had long forgotten the words to it. While most people would have liked to know the words to such a sweet tune, she preferred the emptiness. She once said that some things are best left forgotten so that we can truly appreciate it. Silly girl.

.. .. ..

How long I had been out was a mystery to me as I awoke covered in bandages and swaddled in warm blankets. In fact, I was so swaddled that my initial movement was severely constricted most likely as an attempt to prevent me from rolling over on my wound in my sleep. The room in which I was being kept was a small one with very little to help mitigate its bland appearance, but it was better than still being stuck in that cell, so I quickly came to like the quaint setting. Slowly I tested my body as I tried to sit up and to my pleasant surprise there was no pain. The pain in my chest had virtually all but disappeared, and the rest of my injuries I had suffered prior to that one felt healed as well. I was alive and well which certainly did come to me as a surprise. Before I could contemplate more on my good fortune, Arthur came into the room where I had been situated and offered me some water from his canteen. I snatched the water from him like a hungry child and chugged it down so fast that the excess water that spilled from my mouth soaked my bandages.

I had severely underestimated the state that my body was in for me to have acted in such a way, but when I thought back on it, I had not had a chance to eat since Melwas' little dinner party and I hardly ate anything there out of caution.

Arthur had too received some sort of medical attention, but not nearly as intensive as mine with no surprise.

When I saw him, for a brief moment my heart dropped. I had no idea why at the time, but I suppose that a part of me would have like to see either Galahad or Elaine as the first people to see me instead of some pretend merc I had only met a few days prior. He leaned against the wall as he took a drink as well from the canteen. Despite my preferences on who my visitors, I had to still thank him because I had to surmise that either he or Bors were the ones to bring me to get medical attention.

Even with the water I just drank, my mouth felt a little dry as I spoke, "It seems as though I owe you thanks Arthur."

He looked my way and shrugged, "It was nothing. I was just repaying my debt to you for dragging me around when I was sick…even though that was your fault."

Hmm, he was still a little sore about that. Well as with any repair, the best way to quickly mend it was to just put a loose board to cover the area.

"Bygones, Arthur bygones. After all, we just defeated one of the bandit kings of Cambria, so I 'm sure we can look past our rocky start to celebrate our newest accomplishment."

"You mean you defeated him. I just defeated a dozen of his men that tried to kill you afterward that's all. It really pales in comparison."

Either he was being a real piece of work with his sarcasm, or he genially was that humble and felt that way. Either way I could tell by the uncharacteristic melancholy tone in his voice that something ailed him.

"Look Arthur, it's just like Melwas said: we are not little girls that need to play these little games to discern what the other is thinking. We are men and if something is bothering you then just spit it out."

For the first time since he came in, he shot a look my way, and to be honest I wish he had not. Never before had I seen such a look of distain and disappointment on a man's face. He had made it look like I had killed his dog or something like that.

"How dare you of all people quote that man after you went and desecrated his body and destroyed his dreams. Have you no sense of honor or guilt?"

"Guilt? The man kept me in a dungeon for days and even before that sent men to kill us, so no Arthur I don't feel guilty that I killed him. And honor, I believe that you forgot whom we were dealing with. He was a bandit king of Cambria, one of the most coldhearted and vicious group of people in Britannia. If anything, I did this land a favor by taking him down."

"So you fancy yourself a hero now huh? Well Lancelot did you know now that Melwas is dead that his territory in Cornwall will become a bloodbath between his men as they fight for succession to his seat. Who knows how many innocent villages will be caught up in the chaos…"

That self-righteous little prick.

"I don't seem to recall you having any qualms about killing him when we were held prisoner, so what's your deal now?"

"You didn't see what I saw Lancelot. After hearing Melwas was dead…I had no idea that men could behave in such a way. They were like dogs…"

"That just had their leashes loosened right? Trust me I know the type. So I take it that things got pretty intense after my fight, but what of Bors and Galahad did they make it out alright as well?"

Arthur seemed to want to continue discussing Melwas' death, but I saw no room for compromise so I ended the discussion. Despite the fallout from it, it had to be done regardless.

"Ah yes, the two of them made it out along with me, and just as you requested Bors was able to take Melwas' head along with us as proof of your victory."

His head? Indeed I had wanted to take it to show the Saxons proof of the deed, but I had never instructed Bors to do such a thing. The way that man knew exactly what I am thinking at times is a bit disturbing, but in this case I must praise him for being able to do so especially under those circumstances.

"Good, I'm glad to hear that oaf can do more than just tie knots and can listen to directions. If you may Arthur, can you have them come here?"

"Bors has returned to Bamburgh Castle. He says that he hates these southern lands and since you were going to survive and didn't need him any longer he was going home. Oh before he left he did say that you were welcome to claim your seat whenever you pleased."

Typical Bors. At times I swear he had the mentality of a whore. He was all game to help in a given task, but the moment it was done he went about to his own life without a care or concern. And as for his offer I would only return once I had secured my prize as well.

"I see, so then what of Galahad? I'm sure that things must have been rough on the lad."

My apologies, Lancelot perhaps I should have worded that differently. Galahad was fine by my standards as a warrior, but by the standards of a mother well…"

Elaine. From the tone of his voice, it seemed like Galahad sustained some sort of minor injury, but knowing that woman she probably tried to go on a bigger rampage than Alexander of Macedonia over it.

"I see, did she say where they were going?"

Arthur turned away and sighed as he responded, "No, all she said was good luck with your foolish quest and never seek out her aid again."

Typical of Elaine: always so emotional and dramatic when it came to these sorts of things. For someone that was supposed to be well known informant, she had proved to be surprisingly emotional on many occasions over the time I had spent with her. From what Merlin and the others told me of her craft beforehand, I had half expected to find a woman with a tactless heart whom would only see the world through logic and facts. Instead, the woman that I had gotten to know exhibited none of those traits as well have exuding more of the fallacious tendencies that all women have proven to be prone to. Still, it was nice to have them around this past year again. There was only one time when I asked Mother what a real family, one absolved of an atmosphere of sex and absentee father figures, was like. The only answer I ever got from her was one that was muffled by tears and a stuttering voice. If she had never made it clear before, that day it became painfully clear that she could never provide me with such an environment. Once that realization kicked in, I hardly ever thought of the idea of a *real* family. The family that I had no matter how dysfunctional was the only one I thought I ever needed. The sentiment was a sweet one but a foolish one all the same.

Mother, nor Luciana could ever had provided me the same life and happiness that Elaine was able to give to Galahad .That smile that he grew up with was not one that was painted on in order to please the scumbags that littered the brothel floor all staring at Mother. His smile was one that I would never have. Even during my days with Elaine and Galahad when Luciana seemed not to be as important as she once was, I found myself unable to find the same smile that Galahad had. I may have been able to laugh with them and I was even able to smile alongside them, but that general happiness that they had to just be alive was a missing and foreign feeling to me.

There was only one night when I had thought past what would occur after I saved Luciana because I could not take her back to the brothel, so I had created this illusion of her and I continuing to live with Elaine and Galahad. But now those two were gone, and most likely beyond my reach for the rest of my days. I don't know what came over me to confide in Arthur in such a way. I suppose I must have still been feeling weak from my wounds. But all the same I opened up to him saying, "I understand why she left, I truly do, but I at the very least would have liked to see them all one last time. Was Elaine's rage such that she would purposely deny me that courtesy?"

Arthur seemed amused at first that I actually asked him

a question like that but he answered with the same serious tone as any other time, "It was for the best that they left Lancelot. I don't know what you taught that boy, but whatever it was could not prepare him for the carnage that was unleashed following your victory. There was a moment... when Bors dropped you and some random bandit tried to kill you, but Galahad pounced on him and stabbed him in the heart over and over and over. I had to literally tear him away from the man's body as he screamed more curses to anyone that dared to take you from him. His love for you Lancelot is a great one indeed and seeing you almost die multiple times...it was for the best for him to leave. But if it puts your heart at ease, Galahad was in tears when he left and I believe that Elaine was on the verge as well. The interaction that I had with them was brief, but despite the outcome I could tell they had nothing but love for you"

"Love huh, well once again it seems as though love has found a way to cause me nothing but trouble."

Too much. I had said far too much.

"So is that how you feel about this Luciana? If so it would explain the urgency of this grand quest we have undertaken."

"So is that what this is? A lovelorn warrior has embarked upon this grand quest to save the woman he loves. Well if that's the case I praise the writer of this story for making me such a good looking man."

"More like you should thank him for having me come your way."

"The lovelorn warrior and his silent traveling companion going off for a grand adventure huh. It's a shame that's not how this story was originally made for. Never before have I heard a tale of the hero causing the abduction of his love, running away from her, putting a child he loved dearly in paramount danger, and taking advantage of his mother in a way that even after she leaves that he feels nothing for her! I laid with that woman for months Arthur and…and…I feel sad not because I cared for her, but because I will not have her resources any longer. Is it no surprise that we are in the situation that we are in now for Luciana."

Arthur just stood there in silence for a moment and seemed to take everything in.

"No but I've heard of a hero that laments over the mistakes that he has made. That's the difference between you and those men under Melwas Lancelot. Those men…when they kill and steal and rape they do so out of a sense of greed in their hearts. Despite how…questionable your methods have been so far, they have been done with a heavy heart any man can see that."

"Heavy heart or not, I am now no different from the men that I have looked down upon for all of these times. You say that they did their evil out of greed, but I fall into the same category. I'm sure there are plenty of other girls that those Mercs you are with have captured, but I care not for a single one of them. The only one I want is Luciana. I'm acting not of some noble goal but just as a selfish desire to get this woman back."

"Noble or selfish Lancelot, the fact remains that you have been tearing this land apart trying to save this woman. If there were more people like you in the world, then perhaps we could finally make this land worth something."

"Careful Arthur, you're beginning to sound like Melwas at this rate. People may start to believe that you believe in Camelot as well."

Arthur moved towards the window by the foot of my bed and stared into the distance.

"I never said that I didn't did I. Melwas was simply misguided but his ideal was one worth pursuing."

For a brief moment I thought I must still be dreaming or maybe even dead. I didn't think that anyone outside those barbarians in Cambria could believe in such an ideal, but perhaps Arthur had been affect by the Mercs he's been with thus far.

"So what you wish to have more vigilantes like me running about the country side doing as we please to satisfy our desires?"

"No, I believe people like you can be guided towards the lawful way of doing things as long as you're given something to believe in. You're not the first of your kind that I've run into Lancelot. My own brother Kay shares many similarities with you when it comes to your views. It is apparent to many people in this land that their rulers have failed them and wish to do nothing but line their own pockets and expand the power of the nobility. Once the people lose faith in their governors, the power of the nation as a whole suffers."

"I'm sure that many people Arthur didn't believe in what Rome was doing, but they remained strong for centuries. People are nothing but tools that a nations uses to strengthen its assets. Happy tools are nice, but tools are tools at the end of the day."

"Only a citizen that has been abandoned by its nation begins to feel that way. If Albion had done everything in its power to help Luciana, then I believe that you would have a very different attitude on the matter. The rulers of a nation are as a father over his children. If showered with love and respect, the child will grow to love that father and do as he says. If neglected though, that child will grow to resent his father and then do actions out of spite and disobedience. As long as Uther, and Mark continue to neglect their citizens and allow the nobility to do as they please, the people will rebel and take the justice and law they seek into their own hands. The Camelot that I seek is one that will exhibit these morals and prevent the people from seeking their own justice."

He was right. I can't believe I thought he was right. Every word that he said resonated within my heart and actually caused me to believe what this man had said. Despite the complex societies that people strived to build, people were simple beings that desired to be controlled whether they knew it or not. I wanted to further share my beliefs on his Camelot, but the Mercs from before came into the room with blades drawn.

In an instant, the mood went from a tranquil one in which the seeds of true discourse and perhaps even friendship could develop to a tense one in which I could feel the mounting tension amounting in the room. The pain from my wounds may have been gone, but I still was in no shape to handle six well-armed men that obviously had a bone to pick with us. So for the moment it seemed as though

I was dependent on Arthur getting me out of whatever situation that we had fallen into. The leader of the Mercs came forward with his blade pointed at me as he spoke, "Briton, it's good to see you awake because we have questions for you. Two of my best men I send with you to get your son, and only one has returned. From Cub's story he says that Varna was killed by the likes of you puny Britons that hardly know which side of a sword to kill a man with. Cub is many things but most of all he is a bad liar, so choose your words carefully and tell me what befell my man."

Arthur had his hands tied in this one. I tried my best to think back to Elaine and Galahad leaving, so I could get a firm grip on the emotions I had felt then. I looked at the leader with a blank face and timid eyes that did all they could to dance around making contact with his. I tried my best to sound as strong as I could I told him, "I killed him…I killed Varna. I was so stupid. He told me not to keep pressing forward without taking a break, but I didn't listen and I led us into a trap where he took an arrow to the leg and another one to the side. He fought valiantly despite his injuries and died making sure that Cub and I made it out alive. But make no mistake, I killed Varna with my own impatience."

The leader read my face carefully before he sheathed his blade. I breathed a sigh of relief before the leader snapped at Arthur, "Varna was your partner Cub, so I'll let you kill this man. We fulfilled our contract and helped get his son back, but now he will pay for our brother's life."

My heart came to a dead stop after once those cruel

words left the leaders lips. I wanted to look to Arthur, but I already knew what he would do. His words of Camelot and his mission to save the girls that had been captured by these Mercs ran through my mind once more. If I was in his shoes, then I would kill me without hesitation and I knew he would do the same. The funny thing though was I actually was ok with him killing me. I knew he would save Luciana and Arthur deserved to live much more than I did, and perhaps he may even continue to build this dream of his. He may not have had noble blood, but there was something about him that mad made me believe he could do it. I tried to not think about how this was the end for me. I let my mind roll back to thoughts of Luciana and Mother until I heard Arthur say in opposition, "Kain, this man owes Varna a debt of life and he aided me in killing Melwas the bandit king. I say that we keep him alive and force him to join our group till he dies to truly repay his debt. That way he will die no matter what and at least he will serve us some use as well."

I knew Arthur was a kind soul, but I never thought he was that stupid about it as well. Their leader, Kain, thought on his words for a moment and took another look at me and then one at Arthur as well.

"He will serve as nothing more than a manservant for you and be regulated duties as such. What you do with him for jobs is up to you, but he shall not be considered one of us and he will be your responsibility. "

I looked toward Arthur who shot me a dirty look before he hit me in the face.

"Varna was ten ties the man that you ever will be Briton, so keep that in mind as you continue to cling on to you pitiful life."

A bad liar huh….right. They left Arthur and I alone once more in the room as they went to prepare the supplies for the trip ahead of us. The anxiousness that had built up through my body eased up as I found myself lying back down and looking Arthurs' way. I found myself asking him, "So what's next for us now?"

"What's next? What's next is about a month of stormy waters aboard a ship that was meant to serve as nothing more than firewood, and following that we will disembark on a forgotten land that I doubt that even the Romans knew too much of when they tried to take it."

"Hibernia? That's where the Saxons have set up? Never…I never would have thought that to be possible. That land is essentially uncharted and thought to be cursed. How big is their camp?"

"I have yet to discover these facts, but I do know that all of the people that they have abducted have been sent to that camp on the west coast of Hibernia."

Hibernia…I never in my wildest dreams would have I thought my journey would take me to such a remote location, but it would not be for quite some time till we left for that leg in my journey. My wounds hampered any serious movement and Kain had yet to procure the necessary supplies to guarantee a safe trip for us all. It would be months before we set out, yet I was content with that. For nearly a year I had planned on how to join this group of scoundrels, and now all of my plans had come to fruition and I even had an ally with me as well. I was grateful for my good fortune, but not nearly as I should have been for the next chapter of my life in Hibernia would test my limits and if it wasn't for Arthur I would surly not be recounting this tale.

*Hibernia…that was where Luciana was along side with my unforeseen destiny.*

# Epilogue

When I joined the Saxon ranks, that was when the course of Britannia would shift. So many things have yet to occur, yet I cannot place them all in this one account. Even as I seal these very words on parchment, the seeds of Mordred continue to look for me, and if they succeed they must not be allowed to destroy this history as well. So much proof, so many accounts, so many testimonies have already been erased from this world. I will not be foolish and just place the one final account of what happened in one place for them. My words, my truths, shall be spread across the land and God willing, will one day find the light once more.

*To discover the next truth, one must journey across the sea for the Hibernia Chapters...*

CPSIA information can be obtained at www.ICGtesting.com
Printed in the USA
LVOW08s0304280913

354495LV00001B/2/P